THE HEART of
HENRY
QUANTUM

THE HEART of HENRY QUANTUM

PEPPER HARDING

GALLERY BOOKS

New York London Toronto Sydney New Delhi

G

Gallery Books
An Imprint of Simon & Schuster, Inc.
1230 Avenue of the Americas
New York, NY 10020

First Gallery Books hardcover edition October 2016

GALLERY BOOKS and colophon are registered trademarks of Simon & Schuster, Inc.

For information about special discounts for bulk purchases, please contact Simon & Schuster Special Sales at 1-866-506-1949 or business@simonandschuster.com.

The Simon & Schuster Speakers Bureau can bring authors to your live event. For more information or to book an event, contact the Simon & Schuster Speakers Bureau at 1-866-248-3049 or visit our website at www.simonspeakers.com.

Interior design by Jaime Putorti

Manufactured in the United States of America

10 9 8 7 6 5 4 3 2 1

Library of Congress Cataloging-in-Publication Data is available.

ISBN 978-1-5011-2680-2
ISBN 978-1-5011-2682-6 (ebook)

For M. Gorman and R. Futernick.

If they had known what they were talking about, this book

could never have been written.

And for RDH, my friend and inspiration.

PART ONE

HENRY

CHAPTER 1

December 23rd. 7:35-10:14 a.m.

My friend Henry Quantum, whom everyone called Bones because he was so tall and thin, and because Dr. McCoy was his favorite character from *Star Trek*, had a single task that day, and that was to buy a Christmas present for his wife. Having put this off for several weeks (or months, actually), and having noted with alarm when checking his iPhone for updates from the *Huffington Post* that the twenty-third of December had arrived without the purchase of anything at all, not even a stocking stuffer, he knew he had no choice but to go shopping. It was a workday, so there were a few other things on the agenda, but in terms of mission only one: make Margaret happy. He had already settled on a bottle of Chanel No. 5—and decided where to get it, too: at Macy's; and he also figured that the best time to get it would be first thing in the morning so that he wouldn't have to worry about it the rest of the day. All this he decided in a panic upon waking, but, having made his decisions, a kind of peace descended upon him and he entered the shower with a happy heart. Done, done, done, and done! he told himself.

However, when he reached for the soap his hand froze mid-grab because the water bouncing off his shoulders made him think about the miraculous impermeability of his own skin, and this made him think of the wonder of nature, which, when he thought about it, included the entire cosmos, and thus the Hubble telescope came into his mind and the pictures of the galaxies he had seen at the NASA booth at the Sausalito Art Festival back in September, particularly the Sombrero Galaxy, which actually did look like a sombrero, and this led him to recall something that had been drilled into his head since junior high school, namely that light travels at 186,000 miles per second, and when you look at a distant object, like, say, the Sombrero Galaxy, what you are actually seeing is how the object appeared millions of years ago (in the case of the Sombrero Galaxy, thirty million years) and not how it is now; in fact, who could say what it looked like now? For all anyone knew, it could already be colliding with our own galaxy, because a lot can happen in thirty million years, and when he thought about that, he just couldn't quite reach the soap dish, just as he could never get to the Sombrero Galaxy even if he had the power to transport himself there instantaneously, because the galaxy that he envisioned no longer existed. In fact, *everything* outside of himself was happening in the past—that soap dish, for instance—it was already over, done, finished, kaput, history. He had been a sometime practitioner of Zen and was always going on about living in the present—the breath of the present, they called it—but now he had to admit he could never achieve that goal no matter how hard he tried. No one could achieve it, not even the Buddha himself. He stepped over the lip of the tub, and the velour of the bath mat felt the same as it always did, soft and welcoming, only now he realized it was an illusion. It used to be soft and welcoming, a nanosecond ago. But now? Who knew?

He threw on his robe and marched into the kitchen.

Margaret looked up from her oatmeal and said, "What now?"

He grabbed two slices of whole grain, slid them into the toaster, and watched the coils rouse themselves to brilliant orange. He warmed his palms over the slots. "What if a small star was suddenly created one light-year away from us?" he said to Margaret. "And what if it instantly began traveling toward us at just under the speed of light. What would we see? We'd see a star six trillion miles away, when actually it was almost already here, or maybe, because it was so close, we'd see it big and bright and also small and distant at the same time. But the main thing is, we'd never see it as it is and by the time we figured it out, by the time we knew it had been created, it would be on top of us and we'd all die."

"Would you like regular or decaf?" she replied.

"No, I'm serious," he said.

"I know," she said. "But it's a hypothetical star, isn't it?"

"Yes."

"Then have some coffee first."

He carried his toast to the table and sat down dejectedly.

"Maybe we can worry about something else today. What do you think?" she said.

"It's on my mind."

"I know, but why don't you tell me what your day's like today."

"Oh, I don't know, the usual," he answered cagily, remembering he was going to buy her a bottle of perfume. But then he also recalled he had a client coming in, and he had to present to them the new TV spots at around ten thirty, so he couldn't buy the perfume in the morning and he said, "Shit."

"What?"

"The Protox people are coming in today."

"You'll do fine," she said.

The words "fine" and "Protox" together instantly brought up an image of Denise, the art director, and her tattoos, and he tried to imagine what it felt like to get tattooed, the needle going into his arm, leaving behind lines of orange and blue, but he had no idea if this was really how it was done, whether it was lines or dots or what, or if you had to be drunk or if they let you do it sober, because he didn't like needles, period. And Denise had such thin arms. Whenever he went to have his blood drawn he had to turn his head away because he couldn't stand watching his own blood fill up the vial, and then he wondered how much blood there is in a human being, and the answer is ten pints if you're a man and less if you're a woman, unless you're a big woman, like a weight trainer, and he thought about the muscles on those women and he wondered what it would be like to sleep with a muscle-bound woman, it would be kind of gay-straight, because their breasts do sort of disappear. . . .

"Aren't you going to eat your toast?" Margaret asked.

"Oh. No. You take it. Thinking about Protox."

"It's a disgusting product," she said. "Don't you ever get sick of hawking that crap?"

Here we go, he thought. "It's advertising. It's what I do." But, happily, she let it drop and, instead, leaned over and kissed him on the forehead. "Are you all right now, Bones?" she asked.

"Of course."

"No more planetary catastrophes? Can I be sure that when you come home tonight the world will still be in one piece?"

"Ha-ha," he said.

She gave him one of her slightly condescending smiles and then returned to the *Times*, which she now read electronically.

He went to the bedroom, threw on some slim-fit khakis and a sports coat, decided on the cordovan loafers, checked himself out in the mirror, congratulated himself on the fact his stomach didn't stick out over his pants—which it did on practically everyone else his age, which was forty and some months. He still had a full head of hair, though he checked it every day for signs of thinning and could never seem to get rid of the cowlick that stuck out at strange angles whenever the wind blew. His eyes were a lighthearted blue, some would say dreamy, and Margaret complained that he always seemed to be gazing off into space, which of course he wasn't; he was just thinking. Her kinder friends said he resembled the actor James Stewart—by which they meant gangly and awkward, but he took to mean elegant and pure of heart—and maybe he was both, because he had to admit he could appear a bit discombobulated when he wasn't paying attention to what he was doing.

"Oh well!" he said, and grabbed his briefcase and made his way down to the garage.

They lived on a hillside, so their house was on stilts and their garage was dug into the earth and it reminded him of a bomb shelter, except that it was always damp and smelled of mushrooms. In the winter the ants invaded, and sometimes the back wall was stained with runoff, which made him worry about mudslides. But this year there weren't any ants because it wasn't raining, which meant there was a drought and come summer there could be a fire like the one in Oakland that had burned down a thousand homes. Although fires were actually worse in the summer after a lot of rain, which was ironic, but it was because of all the undergrowth. Some kid throws a match, some idiot knocks over the barbecue, and *whufff*!

Margaret called down from the top of the garage stairs: "Henry, take your scarf, you get chilly. And oh, I forgot to tell you, I won't be home for dinner; you'll be all right, won't you?"

"Of course I'll be all right," he said. "I'm not helpless."

"You sure?"

"Yes, I'm sure!"

She blew him a dry kiss and disappeared back into the house. He stood looking at the door, the one that connected the garage to the kitchen, a portal between their two worlds, and he suddenly felt relieved to be leaving.

"Fuck," he said. "Now I also have to worry about dinner."

———

The car Henry Quantum drove was a BMW 528i. Whenever he stepped into it and smelled the leather, whenever he touched the gleaming wood or glistening plastic of the dashboard, whenever he gripped the thick, supple padding of the steering wheel or the cool brushed aluminum of the gear shift, he believed for a moment in his own success. It was leased, of course, and the five hundred a month was tax deductible, but he was proud to pull into any parking lot or up to any restaurant, and it didn't matter to him that there were thousands of these cars in San Francisco, or that they were a cliché, or that truly successful people drove bigger, fancier cars. Because inside his BMW 528i, Henry Quantum felt contentment, and the time he spent driving from Twin Peaks down to Jackson Square was the best half hour of his day. He wondered if maybe, though, he could squeeze in the perfume before work if he went to Nordstrom instead of Macy's because you can't make a left turn off Market Street and Nordstrom was a right, plus they had valet parking. Speaking of valet, he chided himself that the car needed washing and waxing and he promised himself to have Roberto do it or to even take it over to the Touchless Car Wash himself at some point, and he thought, why do people put things off? Why don't we just do what we say we are going to do? And he wondered if perhaps there was some sort of survival benefit to procrastination, because otherwise, why would we have this trait? He was a firm believer in natural selection. He had just read an article by a guy named Pinsker or Pisker or, oh yes, Pinker, which was an amusing name, because that was also the name of sewing scissors—pinking shears—with a scalloped edge so the material you cut wouldn't unravel, and this led him to think about the idea of invention, because somebody had to come up with the pinking shears and had named them pinking shears, and that was the way it was with just about everything. It was wonderful, just wonderful, because who invented cheese? The first person to make butter—you have to stir that cream a long fucking time to make butter—why would anyone do that in the first place? And yet they did.

And that's the whole human endeavor right there. Then he had to slam on the brakes because the light had turned red and he was about to hit the Honda in front of him.

In a moment, the light turned green again, the Honda lurched forward and so did Henry, now determined to stop daydreaming while driving. When you think about it, he said to himself, people really don't pay all that much attention when they're driving. For instance when you want to change lanes, you are looking in the rearview mirror and still moving forward without looking ahead, and yet somehow you judge your distance correctly 99.99 percent of the time. And what about when you're on the iPhone or texting? He admitted he called when driving, but no texting, at least not that. The truth is, he never quite got that two-thumbs thing down— and as for tweeting, he just didn't do it. Though it was hard to be in advertising and not tweet, because tweeting was maybe the most important medium for targets under thirty.

Shit, he said to himself. Now I have to fucking tweet!

His first tweet would be: *I am on my way to buy perfume for Margaret. Can't decide which store.* Second tweet: *What's the point of Christmas, anyway? Anyone know?* Third tweet: *Just almost hit hot girl on bike. Hate those fucking bike lanes.* He tweeted all this mentally because he was not ready to tweet physically.

He was actually enjoying all this tweeting, until he realized that he'd passed Fifth Street, where Nordstrom was, and hadn't turned. In fact, he was already at the Ferry Building. But he was determined not to get upset, because he was a practitioner of Samatha meditation and also of Taoism, or at least he wanted to be, and since the path of life was pointing him away from Nordstrom, he decided to trust that this was the right way to go even though it was a big inconvenience. Thus he turned left on Drumm past the Bay Club and left again on Jackson—in other words, he went straight to the office. He could get the perfume later. Hoof it over to Union Square during lunch, why not? It would do him good. That's the Tao for you!

He pulled into the garage, cried "*¡Hola!*" to Roberto the attendant, and walked the three blocks to his office on Pacific. It was just up the block from the famous Thomas E. Cara espresso machine store, and also across from where American Zoetrope used to be when Francis Ford Coppola worked there. Every time Henry Quantum walked these three blocks, strolling past the magnificent antiques shops or cutting up the alley past BIX (best martinis in town) or checking out the scene at Roka Bar or the chicks coming out of the law offices or detouring past that crazy combination men's shop/bar/golf simulator/wine cave on the corner of Montgomery and Clay, he was filled with love—love for this little corner of the universe and for the people who lived and worked in it. On this particular morning, just one day before Christmas Eve, the winter light was working its magic—golden yet somehow also porcelain, white and clarifying yet thick with mystery—imbuing the old brick buildings with shimmering vitality and the pedestrians with a healthy glow quite unlike the pallor they wore in those gloomy, foggy summers that felt so gray and damp. Half the people who passed him were bundled in winter coats, the other half in shorts and T-shirts. So San Francisco! Most of the country was freezing, big snowstorms in the Midwest and all, but here the young women, though they sported elegant boots, wore their skirts to the tops of their thighs and let their legs go bare; the young men were all squeezed into hypertight pants and tailored sports coats cut to look two sizes too small; some wore skinny black ties with open collars, some wore sweaters, some wore polos, and some were just in jeans and sneakers. All this gave Henry an oceanic lift, the tide of which swept him along until he reached number 46, yanked open the art deco door with its etched-glass insert, and bounded up the staircase that had been refitted with teakwood and aluminum to resemble nothing so much as the grand lobby of a Disney cruise ship.

Like all the buildings on this quaint block, his was a relic of the old Barbary Coast, a narrowish, three-story brick Italianate that once housed a saloon or a brothel or perhaps a brewery or a dance hall, though now it was painted chalk white and had shutters the color of wild iris. The sign that hung above its door was not HIPPODROME or KELLY'S as in the old days, but BIGALOW, GREEN, ANDERSON AND SILVERMAN, and each time he passed under this sign and said good-bye to the wonderful flow of humanity that swelled his heart, he found himself coughing violently, as if the air inside was carcinogenic, which, in fact, he often thought it was.

"But I'm fine with it," he told himself each morning.

The hour was now nine thirty. Naturally none of the creative department had yet arrived (everyone in account services had been there since seven), and this was perfect because Henry saw himself as inhabiting a privileged station midway between business and creative—he was neither right brain nor left brain—he was all brain, a man for all seasons, a pigeon not to be holed, as he put it at cocktail parties right before whomever he was speaking to found a way to escape. Yes, okay, he had once wanted to be a copywriter—that was ages ago, before he decided he had no talent for the witty line or the powerful metaphor; but he understood creative people—he did—and so he believed his mission was to champion their work to the idiots who paid the bills. That, in fact, is what he had in mind for the Protox presentation—support his creatives even if he hated their work, which in this case he did. This had to do with his samurai ethos.

He set his briefcase on his desk as carefully as if it were a finely honed katana from the hand of Hattori Hanzo, the greatest sword maker of all time, at least in *Kill Bill Volume 1*, and rounding his desk, slowly lowered himself into his Aeron chair, a chair fit for a warrior. For the zillionth time he perused his workspace, which he again found lackluster in spite of the Grateful Dead posters and quotations from Nietzsche and the Dalai Lama hanging on the wall. It was an outer office, yes, and he was proud of that, but it was only eight by ten and it was fronted by a glass wall that afforded him no privacy at all. When he tried to draw the blinds they refused to work, or if they did, people would tap on the window as if it were illegal to have a minute to himself. But honestly, who would want to be closed in this office anyway? The carpet was stained, the desk was mostly composite, and the only natural light came from a small, soot-encrusted window that looked out across a trash-strewn alley to the crumbling rear of a speakeasy on Broadway. He had found himself looking out that window often, and for years tried to spy into the windows opposite his own. Who lives above a strip joint? he wondered. Ratty curtains blocked the view, and some of the windows were papered over with yellowed newspaper. Probably Vietnamese immigrants. Or maybe the bouncer who stands in front of the entrance lives there. Not the worst job in the world. He gets to kibitz with the girls at least.

Henry had gone into one of those strip joints once. It was the cleavage on the young woman who accosted him as he was walking to North Beach for some pasta that had beckoned him in. And yet she spoke to him so gently. "You seem like a nice person," she said. "You do, too," he replied, feeling incredibly stupid the minute the words came out of his mouth. But she smiled and said, "Aren't you sweet!" and parted the curtains and led him inside. It wasn't until he was at a table that they told him the girls wouldn't sit with him unless he ordered a bottle of champagne. But he didn't want them to sit with him. In fact, he wanted to get out, but the girl, still holding his hand, said, "Don't worry. I'll sit with you, no champagne," so he sat. There was another girl onstage dancing lethargically in complete nakedness except for high heels. The one holding his hand spoke with a slight southern accent.

"Used to be, back in the day, like in the seventies or something, we could be nude the whole time. Way before me. Now we have to wear at least lingerie when we sit with the guys."

"Really?" he said.

"Um," she replied.

She couldn't have been more than eighteen. It was all the paint on her face that had fooled him. Christ, he thought to himself, what am I doing? He was suddenly struck by how her makeup stopped so abruptly under her chin. How pale her neck was. And under the pancake, pimples. And then he had a flash of inspiration: he would get her out of there! Out of this terrible life. How? He would marry her! Yes!

Except he was already married.

"Buy me a white wine?" she said.

"Okay," he said.

He ordered her one, but the waitress brought her two. And also two for him.

"Two-drink minimum" the waitress muttered. "Per person."

"I love white wine," the girl said. "Don't you? You know, I can dance for you if you like. A private dance, you know? In the back there are rooms."

"Sorry?"

"Just you and me. Say a hundred bucks."

"Oh!" he said.

"It'll be fun."

"I know this sounds crazy," he blurted, "but I want to get you out of here."

"That's what I'm saying. Private room. Lap dance, strip, it'll be really fun."

"No, that's not what I mean."

"Well, okay, sure, whatever you need. Why not? Only a hundred. A lot of places it's a lot more, believe me. But I like you. In fact, I'll do it for eighty because I really like you. You seem like such a nice guy."

She placed her hand on his leg, ran it up toward his groin.

And before he realized it, he'd bolted from his seat, run out of the darkened club, and found himself standing in the white glare of the street.

Except the bouncer ran after him and grabbed him by the collar. "Hey, man, the bill. You probably want to pay that."

"Oh," said Henry. "Sorry, sorry. I forgot."

"Right."

"No, really, I just forgot."

"It's one-twenty."

"One-twenty?"

"Hundred and twenty."

THE HEART OF HENRY QUANTUM

"For a couple of glasses of wine?"

"That's what it costs. Read the menu."

"They didn't show me a menu."

"One-twenty," the guy said.

"Do you take American Express?" Henry asked.

But the beery scent of that room and the sweat he felt coming off the girl stayed with him for a long time. Even now, as he stood there looking across the yard, he brought to mind that place on her neck where the line of makeup gave way to the real girl—and sometimes he wished he hadn't run away and hadn't already been married, because the two of them—he and the girl—could have started over: a house in the country, a passel of kids, an all-electric vehicle. He placed the palm of his hand upon his grimy little window and tried again to see past the curtains on the upper floor of the strip joint. Poor kid!

But then he heard the door to his office open and he turned to see Denise, the tattooed art director, leaning against the doorframe with an armful of layouts.

"Hey," she said. "You ready?"

"You're here already?"

"Why wouldn't I be?" she replied. "It's almost ten. They'll be here in half an hour. I'm going to go set up."

"Right," he said.

"You okay?"

"Why does everyone always ask me that?"

She went off in the direction of the small conference room, but his eyes did not move from the spot she had vacated. He wondered if people leave a trace of themselves when they rest somewhere—not in the way of perfume or body odor, but in the way of essence, of soul. What if we leave little vestiges of our souls wherever we go? And is the totality of the soul diminished or is it somehow enlarged? This brought to mind a little carved soapstone someone had once given him—his old professor of anthropology at Chicago—from India, though he couldn't recall which dynasty—a tiny little frog crudely carved—from the Maratha period, yes—from northern India, some village, he never knew which, and really he had no idea how old it was, maybe from the seventeenth century, maybe from the eighteenth—and this frog was only as big as the tip of his pinky, and the white of the sandstone had turned muddy and dark where it had been rubbed over and over, especially on the ridge of the frog's back where it glistened with oil from a thousand hands—and when Henry held it in his own hands, when he touched it to his cheek, when he put it to his lips, he got the uncanny sensation he was touching not the frog but all the people who had ever rubbed it for good luck, even down to the fellow who first carved it, and that they had all left traces of themselves just as he was leaving something of himself. What an exquisite feeling that was! To be attached to all those lost lives, those obscure creatures without which this little frog would have no patina. They had lived their lives just as he was living his, the only difference being that he knew his own name and he didn't know theirs. And also they were Indian and he wasn't. Although some of them could have been British.

And then he couldn't remember why he was staring at the doorpost, so he pulled out his laptop, powered it up, waited till the screen opened, clicked on the Protox files, reviewed his notes, closed the lid, and carted his computer with him into the conference room.

CHAPTER 2

10:15–11:45 a.m.

On the way to the conference room he stopped to look in at the IT guy, Larry McPeek, who was busy writing code or maybe just shopping on Amazon, and they said hello to each other and said "Merry Christmas," which everyone had been saying to one another for days now, and so Henry continued down the hall wishing everyone a merry Christmas in a very cheerful voice, but actually he was thinking about Denise, the art director. She wasn't exactly hot, because she had a horsey kind of face, but with the tattoos and the hair extensions and the skin-tight jeans with the bright orange cuffs, she was definitely sexy, a model's body as they liked to say when you had no boobs and were tall and slender with a nice little backside; but it was her hands that got to Henry—

the fingers like eels, long and elastic, as if they had no bones and which she held aloft and widespread when she was trying to make a point, or otherwise squeezed upon her waist at either side when she was standing in the hall. Sometimes she used them as a pillow for her chin when she was listening to music or contemplating the placement of a photograph. No matter what they were doing, these fingers were astoundingly erotic—what would they feel like? he wondered. He knew women hated when men objectified them this way. And he hated that he objectified them. But, jeez, he was a guy. And it was hard, really hard, to change fifty thousand years of objectifying women. *You* try it! he silently cried out to Gloria Steinem, the only feminist he could remember the name of at the moment. Yeah, you try it! And by the way, he pointed out to Ms. Steinem, I am completely aware that Denise has a brain. She's kind of egghead-y actually. So please.

He returned to his contemplation of Denise's lubricious hands but had to ask himself: When did people truly take note of their own hands? For instance, you don't see monkeys wearing rings on their fingers. Not *Australopithecus*, either. Not even *Homo erectus*. No. It must have happened at the same time we started painting and making music and praying to gods. Just forty thousand short years ago. That's when we saw our hands not just as useful but as beautiful.

He thought about the cave paintings at Chauvet, and the film about them, and how art at the very beginning of its existence was so extraordinarily beautiful, and that the world in those days was filled with Rembrandts and Titians, only they didn't know it, they thought they were doing magic, not art, which maybe aren't so different after all, and he wondered what those first artists would think of the work Denise did, and this led him again to wonder at her tattoos. Modern primitive, they called it. But she wasn't primitive, was she?

When he entered the conference room he was pleased to notice that Denise had lots of rings on, including a very large one that covered two fingers.

How far we've come! he thought. One ring, two fingers!

He opened his computer and sat himself down next to her with a nonchalant smile. Meanwhile, Alan Schwartz, the associate creative director, came in, sat down on the other side of her, only much closer, and threw his arm around her chair and announced, "We're gonna rock 'em this morning, ain't we?" Alan was educated at Stanford, but he used bad grammar to prove he had street cred.

"It's da bomb!" Henry agreed. "We're gonna pimp that hustle, bro."

"Jesus," said Denise.

Laid out on the table were drawings of people using Protox. They represented the most impossible optimism Henry could imagine. The first was a cute spot with Jennifer Lawrence extolling the virtues of Protox. Next was Chris Froome, the winner of a couple of Tours de France, who counted Protox "team member number one!" Then Tom Brady of the New England Patriots explaining to his supermodel wife how Protox can turn beautiful skin "into *Perfect* with a capital *P*." And the tour de force? Brad Pitt, who, according to Schwartz, has notoriously bad skin, taking the six-week "Beauty Really Is Skin Deep!" cleanse, on camera, 24-7. Together, these people would have to be paid around fifty million dollars. (Not counting the one in which Robert Downey Jr., in full Iron Man regalia, confesses that clearer skin gave him the confidence to get off cocaine and "back into saving the world again. Thank you, Protox!" and then does a tap dance with Gwyneth Paltrow.) Henry knew none of this could ever happen. The budget was six hundred thousand dollars including talent, shooting, editorial, music, special effects, graphics, travel, meals, and the agency's 18.5 percent profit.

"Boy, these look good," he remarked, as Denise gathered up the storyboards and set them facedown upon the rail.

There were also, of course, more realistic approaches. Backup, they called them. But they weren't going to show them unless they absolutely had to.

"You know what?" Henry had said. "Might as well show everything. That way they can see how great the recommendation really is."

When the time came, Henry made a brief introductory presentation and then got lost in his own head for most of the rest of it, having become obsessed with the varieties of fish you could no longer get in the market and the whole business about acid rain and tuna. Occasionally he awoke and jotted down some notes. Finally came the time for client feedback. He looked up from his computer, eyes bright with interest, and said, "So? What's the verdict?"

The clients had been laughing at the scripts in all the right places and had listened attentively to the rationale for each of the campaigns. They'd nodded at the appropriate times and took notes whenever a research fact was mentioned. But now it was their turn. Gretchen, the VP of marketing—the senior person at this particular meeting— looked to her right and her left, found the most junior person in the room, and said, "Albert, what are your opinions?" Albert said that the work was very creative and he really

liked the spot where they were all singing, but he was disappointed that it didn't rhyme.

"It's a work in progress," Denise chimed in.

"Even so," he said.

And then, looking back and forth at Gretchen, he began to point out the deficiencies in each and every spot, always, however, counterbalanced with a nod to their strengths, because Albert apparently couldn't quite tell what Gretchen thought about them.

Next came Pat. Pat was feisty. There was always a feisty one, and in this case it was Pat. With the instinct of a cobra, she tore into the fifty-million-dollar campaign. Aside from being "a bit too expensive," it was something she had seen before, at least a million times.

"You've seen a spot with Iron Man doing a tap dance with Gwyneth Paltrow?" Alan Schwartz asked.

"That's not what I mean. I mean the idea of it."

Well, of course she was right, Henry thought. It *had* all been done before. But hasn't everything? They say there are only seven basic plots in literature—but so what?

Then Ralph, the second-in-command, began his spiel. He was soft-spoken and measured and had a way of making everyone fall asleep after two sentences. He went methodically through each commercial, at each step asking, rhe-

torically it turned out, "How does this realize the strategy? That's my benchmark. How does this realize the strategy? Does this realize the strategy? I look for the strategy in each part, in each line, and I ask myself, does this realize the strategy? And finally, does it, overall, communicate the strategy? In other words, is it strategic?" Of the Tour de France spot, he said, "Isn't the guy Italian or something? Is that strategic? Do Italian bike riders forward the strategic goal? I'm not sure. I'm just not sure."

"He's British," said Schwartz.

"Yes, but is that strategic? This is what I'm asking."

Finally it was Gretchen's turn. She was about fifty years old, which was actually quite old for this job. By fifty she should have at least been an executive VP and not just a brand VP, but she was an idiot and there was nothing she could do about it.

"Well!" she said with a bright and somewhat off-putting smile. "I don't really have much to add. I guess we're not quite there yet. Why don't we take another stab at it? Excellent work, everyone!"

And just then, Frank Bigalow, Henry's boss, the one with his name on the door, popped his head in. "Anyone for Michael Mina?" he said, meaning the clients, not the staff. But then he added, "Quantum, you want to join us?"

"Can't," said Henry, half truthfully. "I have an appoint-ment. But enjoy yourselves!"

And off they went to spend about eight hundred dollars on lunch.

In the emptiness that followed, Henry Quantum announced that he would write up a meeting report and do a new creative brief, and with great enthusiasm told them the work was brilliant and the clients were just Philistines.

Alan Schwartz stood up. "Did you see the look on Gretchen's face? We might as well have been reciting *Finnegans Wake*."

When he left, Denise gathered up the layouts. "Alan needs to feel his work means something."

"What a shame," quipped Henry, which to his surprise elicited a gay laugh from Denise. He had been serious.

In any event, Denise took off a minute or two later and Henry was left alone with his laptop. He looked at his watch. Eleven thirty. He would do a couple of little housekeeping things on his computer and then go get the perfume. The housekeeping had to do with the notes for Protox and how to make the client's idiotic comments cogent. He sighed.

Henry felt honor bound to do his best for Protox, as he would for any client, though as he sat there he had to ask himself why.

For instance, he always insisted creative make it clear that Protox was not a Botox rip-off but an entirely different product. You drank it, it cleansed your system and made your skin glow. That was the basic selling proposition: *Drink your way to younger-looking skin.* Did Protox live up to that claim? Well, if you looked at the before-and-after photos you would certainly think so. But what was rarely (never!) mentioned is that you would always be running to the bathroom. Especially during the three-day super cleanse. Basically, Protox was a laxative.

But you *had* to believe in your clients' products, didn't you?—believe with your whole being, like Billy Graham believed in Jesus: you had to give yourself up to it or you just couldn't get to the promised land. But Henry had been trained as a philosopher, and this was becoming more and more of a problem. Because anyone who has ever read Plato knows that Socrates taught that there are philosophers— and then there are sophists. A philosopher seeks truth. A sophist merely wants to convince you of his argument.

Henry sat looking at the notes he had been typing on his screen. "I am a sophist!" he cried aloud. It was like a blade inserted into his femoral artery and pushed all the way up to his heart. He clutched his stomach. I'm a fucking sophist! All my brainpower, all my persuasive talents, all of *me,* in the service of a laxative! The reason your skin glows is that you are totally dehydrated and feverish.

And what about the other crap I've worked on? Malcolm T. Farnsworth Trousers That Fit. Fit? They didn't fit! They were shit. And soup, he said to himself, I wrote reams and reams on the benefits of canned soup. Not even Campbell's. Some off-brand called Health Country. Should have been Death Country. Cans of salt and sugar is what they were. Cans of liquefied chicken from chicken concentration camps! But the worst was not even the soup or the Protox. It was the Samurai Brand Real Beef Chewing Jerky and Pinch of Beef. Grotesquely processed from the lowest-quality desiccated meat, it was shredded to look like chewing tobacco or powdered to look like snuff, and packaged that way for little kids. Not only was he selling children a food item that was grossly unhealthy, but he was glorifying chewing tobacco! And he had done it with pleasure, with passion, with the true belief of a convert. In fact, if you asked him even now, in this very second of self-flagellation, he would have told you the commercial they made was great. They got a CLIO for it!

It was a music video of a Samurai warrior rapping while flying through treetops and battling the demons of boring snacks. It had a million hits on YouTube in less than a week and the product flew off the shelves—until someone discovered the packaging was faulty and the stuff was sprouting a green halo of incredibly odiferous mold. He remembered the emergency meeting of the account group. "It could have killed someone!" he'd said. But Bigalow, the boss, laughed. "Don't worry about it, Henry," he said. "I made sure they paid in advance."

Now, sitting alone in the conference room, he sighed for the hundredth time that day.

Nobody did actually die, he reminded himself. Most mold is basically benign, isn't it? Penicillin, that's mold. And blue cheese.

He was heartened by the fact that advertisers don't actually lie about stuff. That would be illegal. We just don't tell the whole truth.

After all, the truth is always thick with complexity. Like gumbo. You kind of have to dig through it—and what do you find? Okra.

And then he thought: Why exactly *am* I buying Margaret a bottle of Chanel No. 5? Will that express my true feelings? Or is it just another sales pitch? Just making myself look good. *My true feelings*, he repeated, feeling some sort of door slam, some sort of door that said, "Don't go in there, buddy," some sort of door he most likely always thought would be wide open. Margaret wasn't much on public affection, never was. But lately she'd been offering her cheek instead of her lips for their good-night kiss. Obviously, he was in the doghouse. He just didn't know why. And he'd been in there a long time. A very long time. When he thought about these things he got the strangest sensation in the back of his throat, as if he were coming down with something.

He made his way back to his office looking rather downcast. Here and there he heard a "Merry Christmas" but didn't respond. He sat down, plopped his head onto the desk, not cradled in his arms, just flat on the surface—a surface that wasn't even wood—and closed his eyes. Wood would have smelled nice, like a carpentry shop; it might have soothed him, comforted him—but this material, whatever it was, only alienated a person. No wonder we're so disconnected from ourselves, he thought.

Why had he waited so long to buy her a gift? he wondered. He could remember tons of Christmases—the excitement of planning and shopping, the thrill behind every bow and piece of tape on the wrapping, the joy of watching it all being torn apart—and then, inevitably, the muted, "Oh.

Okay. Nice. Thank you." And the gift, so lovingly chosen, never to be seen again. Had it always been that way? He tried to remember.

There was that first Christmas in San Francisco, wasn't there? When he had lain awake several nights trying to figure out the perfect present. Couldn't think of a thing, of course. Maybe a ring would be nice—but you don't get your new girlfriend a ring, for crying out loud. Could be totally misinterpreted! What about a blouse? Your *mother* buys you a blouse! Shoes? Way too weird, even though he liked shoes. Not to mention everything in Berkeley was so tie-dyed or fair-trade or Athleta or, well, just too head-shop-y for Margaret, which now made him realize that maybe the person he thought she was back then (soft, cuddly, easy to please, and left-wing) she already wasn't, because if she were he would have just bought a bottle of patchouli and been done with it. Instead, he felt compelled to hop on BART and tunnel into San Francisco. Much less tie-dye in Union Square, he reckoned.

"May I help you?" said the first saleslady.

"Just looking," he replied rather tremulously.

"May I help you?" said the second.

"Just looking," he said again, this time with a hint of brio.

And to the third, the fourth, and the fifteenth, he now quite confidently replied, "Just looking!"

And in truth it was hard to choose. Everything he wanted was too expensive. Everything he could afford sucked. But on he shopped, amazed and confused and delighted by the choices the world of commerce provided: A purse? A pair of gloves? A pocket camera? A pair of earrings? Until finally he had the temerity to walk into Shreve.

"Just wondering," he said, nonchalantly tapping on the glass display case, "how much is that one—no, not the ring!—that other little thing—the one with the green stones? Yes that one. What is that exactly?"

It was presented upon a black velvet pallet. "It's called a choker," explained the salesman. "Beautiful, isn't it?"

"It really is."

"Eighteen-karat gold. Almost half a carat of stones." The man delicately flipped over the little ticket that had until now been hidden from view. "Oh! A very good price!" he exclaimed.

"Really?"

"Oh yes. You're really in luck. Just $1,129."

"Wow," said Henry Quantum.

"Wow is right! I almost wonder if it's been mismarked. But she'll love it. Believe me."

"She would. She totally would. It's practically our first Christmas together."

"It's exquisite."

"But I'm just—"

The salesman suddenly placed the necklace in Henry's hand. It flowed over his palm and through his fingers like a glittering waterfall. It had looked so solid in the display case, but actually it was slinky and articulated, like the tail of a dragon whose scales were fashioned of pure gold, and it was heavier than he imagined, too, so he allowed himself to test the heft of it, though he still didn't dare touch the stones. They glimmered in the light coming up from the display case like a swarm of brilliant green fireflies.

"Irresistible," said the salesman.

"How—how much did you say?"

"And if she doesn't absolutely fall in love with it, she can always exchange it," he went on.

"No," Henry murmured. "She'll love it."

And the word "love" seemed to glow from the little green stones with a profound inner light: the word itself, "*love.*" The letters condensed into magic clouds under his feet and lifted him off the hard tile floor, and while he was floating there, he noticed that the entire jewelry store had become quite fuzzy and maybe a little pink.

But here his memory grew a bit dim because he couldn't precisely recall reaching into his pocket, taking out his newly minted credit card, his first, a $1,400 limit, and handing it to the sales clerk. That he did not remember.

But he did remember how Margaret gasped, how she cried, how she practically swooned, how she wrapped herself around him and held herself there for what must have been ten minutes. Not kissing, just holding. Perhaps it was at that moment he realized she might never let go, never ever, and that from this point on there might be a lifetime of holding, a lifetime in which one could, at last, breathe and sleep.

It all came flooding back now: Christmas Eve aglow with little candles and sparkling tinsel, cheap wine in paper cups, and ham she'd baked from a can. They tore into all the other little gifts—the ones she'd given him—long before that Christmas morning on which they'd overslept because they'd made love all through the endless night.

Or maybe they hadn't. He couldn't be sure anymore.

CHAPTER 3

11:46 a.m.–12:38 p.m.

He must have fallen asleep, because the next thing he knew Gladys, the receptionist, was standing over him whining, "Did you turn off your phone again? I've been buzzing you."

Gladys, in spite of her name, was very young and pretty, and this might have been her first real job. She was a graduate of Brown; he didn't know what she'd majored in, probably Italian literature of the late cinquecento or something like that, but for some reason she wanted to break into advertising. Too late, he thought. Advertising is over. TV, radio—pretty much finished. Everything was online now, guerilla, they called it, viral. You had to appear as if you weren't advertising in order to advertise. Yet another fucking layer of subterfuge. But Gladys had a gorgeous, athletic body and straight, limpid, blond hair, which Henry hoped was her natural color but knew in his heart wasn't. Too many highlights and lowlights. He had learned those terms from Denise when he'd brought up the subject of Gladys's beauty. Denise was quick to point out these and several other faults, which gave Henry the feeling she was perhaps marginally interested in him. But right now it was Gladys and her athletic body that was near him, and the refreshing scent of soap she carried with her.

"Oh, sorry," he said, wiping a tendril of spit from the corner of his mouth.

"It's your wife," she explained. "It seems important. She called three times."

"Oh!" he said. "Shit."

"She's on the line now."

He had, in fact, turned off all his phones—his cell and his landline. He hadn't wanted to be interrupted before the meeting or during the meeting or after the meeting, for that matter. The pressure of another human being's words was just a little more than he could handle. Especially Margaret's. Nevertheless, he put the receiver to his ear and said, "Hi, babe."

"Why do you always shut off your phones?" she began.

"I don't know," he said.

"It's so fucking rude."

"Sorry."

"But you always do it."

"Not always."

"Always."

There was no answer to this, so he said, "What's up, hon?"

"It's my brother."

"Oh God. What now?"

"I invited him for Christmas."

"Really?"

"I had to, Bones. He called in tears. That woman has left him."

"Again?"

"He's a mess."

"He's an alcoholic, Margaret."

"No, he's not!"

"He is, but whatever," said Henry, bending a paper clip between his fingers.

"He's just coming for a few days. Don't worry."

Henry sighed yet again, or rather, stifled a sigh. Because a sigh would have communicated what he thought, and he wasn't going to say what he thought. When he'd mentioned the obvious—the substance abuse—she'd already jumped down his throat. And since she would get her way anyway, why bother?

"Maybe you could pick him up at the airport?" she said.

"Me? What about you?"

"I told you I have dinner plans tonight. I can't break them. It's work."

"He's coming *tonight*?"

"I put him on a plane."

"We're paying?"

"Bones!"

"Christ," he said. "Whatever. Just e-mail me the details."

"Thanks, honey," she said.

"Yeah, whatever."

"Believe me, it'll be fine."

"Right."

"Love you!"

"Yeah. Love you, too."

Now he really did sigh. He checked his watch again. It was noon. Get the fucking perfume, he heard himself say.

So he put on his sports coat and tucked his scarf around his neck and walked down the hall to reception, where Gladys asked him, "Are you all right?" and he answered, "For God's sake, yes!" and he bounded down the teak staircase and pushed open the frosted glass door and found himself back on Pacific Avenue. It used to be the biggest whorehouse street in the West—and guess what? It still was!

Perfume, he reminded himself, perfume. And Macy's was his goal. Or he could have lunch first.

If he turned west, he'd be in Chinatown in two seconds, delicious, or he could turn up Columbus and find himself in North Beach, calzone! But sometimes you just have to choose the harder path. He decided he would trek to Union Square, a good twenty-minute walk, and go to fucking Macy's to buy fucking perfume for his fucking wife. Scowling, he crossed Columbus, walked up to Grant, and made his way south through Chinatown, ignoring all the wonderful aromas emerging from all the wonderful restaurants and hoping against hope that he could get through all this and reach the Chinatown gate on Bush Street without so much as a steamed bun. Then he could head over to Geary, where he'd hang a right and end up at Macy's, job complete! As he mapped out his route, it occurred to him how amazing it is that he, or anybody for that matter, could remember how to get from one place to another. There's a map in your head, he thought. You don't even have to plan it all out—you just have to let one foot follow the other and you'll get there; it's practically autonomic, like breathing. It was beautiful, the intricacies of the human body. The flow of blood through the veins and arteries, the electrical signals that jump from one synapse to the other, and the fact that our bodies are really composed of billions, maybe trillions, of separate life-forms, bacteria, viruses, amoebas, and who knows what else, all swarming within you, a living, walking macrobiotic zoo! He marveled at all the other people walking, too, going somewhere as if it were the easiest thing in the world—even tourists who in fact had no idea where they were going and did indeed need real maps—and yet didn't. The mind is just a kind of electronic map anyway, a map of memory and emotion, a map of love and desire, a map of resentment and fear. That's why most of the time he did love advertising— because he was reading a map of untapped need. And also an intellectual map—you mapped out your strategy, didn't you? And using that map, you created pictures in people's minds and souls, images of fulfilled desire and familial happiness that were more real than reality itself; and if people's lives were far from perfect, still, they had this map of perfection, a map that he, Henry Quantum, had placed in them. And now, passing by in every direction, his minions of map readers marched through Chinatown, and he loved each and every one of them, even the very fat ones in their World's Best Mom sweatshirts, and even the sullen teenagers who walked ten paces ahead of their parents pretending they were alone, and even the screaming little ones who were totally out of control and who on any other day would deserve to be sent to toddler reform school, and even, yes, the gay-bashing, survivalist dads in their knock-off Ralph Laurens—he loved them!

He was, however, forced to stop at Red Blossom Tea because he could not resist the scent of jasmine that emanated from the open transom and thought about going in for a tasting and a snack, but, no, he held himself in check. Discipline! Perfume! At Eternity Fine Jewelry he was enchanted by the collection of bright gold thingies in the window—innumerable rings and necklaces and all manner of bejeweled knickknacks. He could buy Margaret a brooch or something—so much cheaper here—but she'd never want anything from a Chinatown jeweler and he'd have to put it in a Tiffany box and she'd find out sooner or later and then it would be worse than buying nothing at all. Macy's! he cried. Perfume! He walked on. But merchandise was spilling onto the narrow sidewalks: cheap plastic fans and fake satin slippers, elaborated back scratchers, sacks of lychee, finely embroidered tablecloths, old-fashioned Chinese hats like they wore when building the transcontinental railroad, traditional Chinese dresses in glimmering red silk, intricately carved ivory dioramas, and huge blue-and-white porcelain urns—it was endless; it was magnificent. What a culture! he thought. In a few years China would own the world. Of course, we used to think that about Japan, he remarked to himself. And look what a mess they are. He wondered why it was that there were all these races of humans in the first place. Was it the amount of sun? You know, in Africa dark skin takes the sunshine better and in Sweden white skin is sort of like snow—but why are the Chinese yellow? Of course they weren't really yellow! Who decided to call them yellow? They were kind of tan, a very pretty shade of tan actually. Ecru. The sun couldn't account for ecru, could it? Because China is both desert and mountain and in some places it's hot and in some places it's frigid. And if there really were races, how come they interbreed? But there was no question about it, most people felt more comfortable with people who looked pretty much like themselves. Although that was changing, too, and, really, was there any person more beautiful than a Eurasian? Let's face it, mongrels are the healthiest, not thoroughbreds. He himself was German, Polish, Irish, and something else, maybe Sioux or Cherokee—in other words, what difference does it make? Sometimes, though, he wished he was from Papua New Guinea, climbing coconut trees with his bare feet and hunting monkeys with a bow and arrow and having communal sex with all the women in the camp.

When he next looked up, he had safely passed through the Chinatown gate and was standing on the corner of Grant and Bush, looking across the street at Café de la Presse, which was also quite delicious. The town was bustling with shoppers. And because it was sunny, Café de la Presse had set out two rows of tables on the sidewalk, and so had the wine bar two doors down and the tables were full. People were filing in and out of stores and up and down the avenues with shopping bags of every color. Some were in couples—gay, straight, young, old, mothers with daughters—and some were alone, but everyone seemed to be dancing to the same happy beat as if the city were keeping time beneath their feet. He walked down to Sutter Street and decided to turn there instead of up Geary—so quickly do plans change—because he wanted to move with the flow of these people, but just as quickly he changed his mind again because he remembered he wanted to go past Prada on the corner of Maiden Lane. He'd been to Prada in Florence, and also to the outlet in Montevarchi, where Margaret bought stuff totaling many thousands of dollars because, she said, "Oh, Bones, it's so cheap!" He almost bought himself a pair of shoes for about $400, which he was told was 75 percent off, but he couldn't do it. Not because of the money, but because there was something unseemly about the pointed toes. Anyway, Prada was now in San Francisco and maybe something from there would be better than perfume, so that's why he kept walking down Grant Avenue. And that's why what happened next happened next.

He had just arrived in front of SlinkyBlink, a new pop-up for hip women's clothing, when someone called out his name.

"Bones!"

He turned around.

"Bones, it's you! Oh my God!"

"Daisy," he heard himself say.

"Oh my God, Bones! I can't believe it! You look great!"

"I do?"

"Delish! A sight for sore eyes!"

She smiled up at him with wide, voluptuous eyes.

"It's nice to see you, too," he said, wondering how long it had been. Three years? Five? Not five. Four.

"Last-minute shopping?" she asked.

"Yeah. For Margaret."

"Of course, of course," she said.

Now, finally, he decided to take a better look at her. Truly he had tried not to, tried not to look at her, but she was standing right in front of him and already her scent, whatever it was she used, had invaded his nostrils. So he allowed his eyes to travel up from her booted toes where he had tried to keep them focused, across her salmon-hued Jackie Kennedy coat with its oversized coral buttons and its rounded schoolgirl collar, up over her long, bare, slender neck, past the curve of her chin to the thick, moist, radiant lips, and then past her upturned nose to those wide, blinding, sea-green eyes, and finally the wild, feathery tips of her auburn hair that peeked like hungry birds from beneath her stylish fur hat. She was dressed as if it were really cold outside, but he knew it was just that she loved fashion and autumn was the most fashionable time of year—though winter had already officially begun. When we say "looked up," really we mean "looked over," because she was much shorter than Henry, petite, but with a fulsome-ish body—not fat, not fat at all—it's just her breasts were a tad larger than her frame would suggest, which gave the impression of her being short-waisted—which she wasn't.

She was beautiful, in fact. Beautiful and adorable and full of life. And that was the problem. He didn't want to remember how beautiful and adorable and full of life she was. He certainly didn't want to allow any inkling of confusion to enter his body, confusion of the extramarital type, which in truth had already begun its torturous journey up his spine. He forced himself to look past her to the store window across the street.

"Hey, kiddo, have you written that novel yet?" she was saying.

"What? No, no, " he chortled.

"You will," she replied, turning serious. But then she smiled. "I broke it off with Noah."

He had no idea who Noah was. "I'm sorry to hear that," he said.

"Don't be," she said. "He turned out to be a complete asshole. All he wanted was sex and television. And wine. He fell asleep every night watching the Shopping Channel. I swear to God. But guess what? I'm getting my PhD after all. Yes, little old me! Neuroscience! Just like we talked about, remember? I'm at SF State. I'm studying the eye. You know, how light signals are perceived on the cellular level. I love it."

"Really?" he said.

"It's because of you, Bones," she continued. "Because you encouraged me. You were the only one who believed in me."

"Me?"

"Of course you."

"Huh!" he said.

"So everything good with Margaret?" Daisy offered up her biggest, most intoxicating smile.

"Great!" he replied.

"I'm glad for you."

"Yeah, really. Great."

"No kids yet?"

"Not yet. Ha-ha! Maybe later."

"Tasha's in fifth grade. Can you believe it? And Denny is starting high school next year!"

"Wow," he said.

"Yeah."

They stood there in front of SlinkyBlink and looked at each other for what seemed a very long time, but it was really only two or three seconds, and then Daisy whispered, "I still collect teddy bears."

"You do?"

"Yeah. It started with you, remember? Whenever we had a night together, you brought one."

"Not every time."

"You used to name them, remember? We had Lost-Weekend Bear. Night-at-the-Opera Bear. One-Month-Anniversary Bear. Remember?"

"You still collect them?"

"Yep."

"Why?"

"Who knows?" She glanced at her watch, "Oh, jeez," she exclaimed. "I have to buzz."

"Yeah, me, too."

"It was great seeing you," she said. "Really great."

"Yeah, it was," he agreed. "Merry Christmas!"

She started to walk away, then came back. "I'm really sorry," she said.

"For what?"

"That I hurt you."

"Oh, come on—"

"No, I am. I'm really sorry."

"It's okay," he said. "I'm sorry, too."

"You have nothing to be sorry for," she said. And then she lifted herself up on her toes, placed a feather-soft kiss upon his cheek, and hurried off in the direction of the Sutter-Stockton Garage.

CHAPTER 4

The world suddenly became quite silent for Henry Quantum. He stood quite still and watched Daisy fade into the crowd. He thought he could just make her out as she found her way into the entrance of the garage, but really he couldn't. Even so, he remained there watching. Was he waiting for her to change her mind and come back to him? There was certainly a time he would have hoped for that. Now it was just—what? Curiosity? Nostalgia? He couldn't put his finger on it, only that his insides had become a bit unsettled.

The last time he'd seen her she was also walking away from him, but that time she was racing into her house, and it was summer, and it was four years ago, and she was wearing her very short cutoffs, and all he could think of at that moment was that he would never be able to touch those fabulous legs again—but even before she entered the house Henry had thrown the BMW in reverse and tore out of her driveway. Surely that meant he didn't really love her. Surely that is not the thing you think when you lose someone you love—I'll miss your legs! And yet he had felt for so long that he had been madly in love with her, couldn't live without her, met her every chance he could, anywhere he could, coffee in Sausalito, sex at the Hilton downtown, and later, when they became very bold, at her house, in her marriage bed, when her husband was off on one of his endless business trips and her children asleep down the hall. Did he feel regret for his transgressions? No, he did not. She even accused him: "Don't you feel the slightest bit guilty?" When he told her the truth, "No, I don't," she shook her head sadly. But he didn't feel guilty, because when he was with her he felt genuine for almost the first time in his life, as if a storm had broken upon him and swept him into a great sea of feeling. The same sudden rain he felt overwhelm him just now. It was like what happens when you are born again, he thought. Deluged in light. Hallelujah! But eventually Daisy's scruples won the day and she broke it off with him, and, in all honesty, he was relieved. He went back into his marriage as if none of it had ever happened. Everything else fell back into place, too. His job. His workouts at the gym. His morning news. His evening novel. He never saw her again. Never even Googled her. Didn't even look her up on Facebook. Margaret never knew, thank God.

But now he wanted more than anything to understand what was happening in his marriage to Margaret. Why had he done what he had done with Daisy? It was strange, his behavior. Unsettling. Unethical. Completely out of character. Never before. Never after. He shuddered even to think of it. But Daisy— Oh, Daisy!

He decided he ought to remember how he and Margaret had first met and how they fell in love and why they were together in the first place. He wanted to remember it exactly, the first time he'd seen Margaret. Yes. He'd spotted her from a block away—she was waiting in line at some restaurant, he couldn't remember which, in Berkeley, probably on Shattuck. He'd only just arrived in San Francisco, having finished college a month before, had already been accepted to graduate school in Chicago, wasn't even remotely thinking of staying in California, certainly wasn't looking for a girlfriend. But there was something about her, must have been, because it emboldened him—maybe he was drunk or stoned, but he didn't think so. It was her, something about her. And the force of that something allowed him to drag his friend Rudy along as he marched right up to her and commenced talking as if he did this kind of thing all the time. What exactly had he said, anyway? He had no idea. But he was in the flow, that's for sure, and whatever it was, it worked. She was enthralled. He felt so powerful and attractive and cool. What was it about her, he wondered now— was it simply the way she stood with those rigid shoulders and slightly arched back? Or the way she was talking to her friend in little whispers as if imparting the most profound secrets, her lips quivering in her friend's ear? Something enigmatic, that's what it was—a straight arrow all closed in on herself with her arms folded and her chin down, but even from a distance he could feel that her eyes were wild and uncontained, two fiery daredevils constantly moving, watchful, ready. And her hair—she'd pulled it into a tight, prissy bun, but strands kept falling out all over her face, as if they too could not be tamed. For some reason he found the schoolmarm outer shell sexy, no question about it. But what he really wanted was the feral creature within. Or at least that's what he told himself.

She had worn glasses back then, wire rims, very intellectual, even though she wasn't in the least, and an Indian skirt down to her ankles, and, my God, Birkenstocks! It's not possible, he thought—had she really looked like that? My tailored Margaret with a dozen pairs of Jimmy Choos and the manicured chestnut hair cut fashionably short in an asymmetrical bob so severe it reminded him of a wedge of cheese? Once, she was rounded and soft. Now she was all angles and edges. She even seemed taller, five seven, where not all that long ago he could have sworn she was five five. Could he be remembering someone else?

The next thing he recalled was his shock when Margaret first took off her clothes in the rather run-down room she rented as a house share. He remembered peeling paint and water-stained floors but also the scent of lavender and roses coming from dozens of sachets she had piled in a basket, and there were fluffy pillows on her bed, the bed he was lying upon when she undressed right before his eyes. And him thinking: this only happens in the movies. And his amazement that under all that crazy, flamboyant, excessive material was a truly beautiful body—slender, proportioned, the skin of an angel, breasts like Aphrodite's on that sculpture he saw at the Met—high, round, smooth—she was perfect, really. But it was how she had stood there waiting nervously for his judgment and how he could not speak, not a word, and how she thought he was displeased—that is what caught him off guard. All he could do, so dumbfounded was he, was spread his arms as wide as he could, and when she fell into them, when he closed them around her and felt her sumptuous skin beneath his hands, he was lost.

Even that day, that first day, she said, "I think you should clip your nails more. Toes, too. Kind of disgusting."

Very soon after that, she started picking out his clothes.

And yet he remembered how dependent on him she became, how she'd clung to his elbow and to his words, too, and how uneasy that made him. He encouraged her to be more independent, to have a more realistic assessment of her abilities and charms. And then one day, she did. This was after the stint in graduate school in Chicago. They'd come back to San Francisco because it was where their best days were and they'd been looking at houses—not that they could afford yet to buy one, but they liked to go to open houses on weekends, playing the role of a successful young couple—when one day she started actually listening to what the agents were saying and how they approached potential clients and how they hooked someone in. "I can do that," she declared as they drove back to their little apartment in their used VW. "Do what?" he asked. "Do what the real estate agent does. How much money do you think they make? I think they make a ton." So she took a course, got an entry-level job, passed the agent's exam, and before he

knew it, she was a different person. It was as if a light had been switched on and she was ablaze. But not toward him. That was the problem. She had this toggle switch in her soul and it could only be on in one direction. He could feel her presence in that darkened state, but could never quite touch her. An infinity of space, that's what it was. A vacuum. Yet space, he reminded himself, was never really empty—it teemed with secret energies and ineluctable particles always in motion. That must have been what he felt all those years. The radiation emanating from her disdain, the dark energy of her contempt.

He was suddenly very glad Daisy had walked away just now. Don't have to deal with *that*, he thought. Perfume for Margaret. Perfume! So he set off again down Grant Avenue and when he reached Geary he turned west toward Union Square. But right there on the corner in front of Peter Panos, the Gentleman's Tailor, a man was playing the saxophone. He was playing a Christmas medley over a recorded soundtrack that blared from two huge speakers festooned with red ribbon and plastic wreaths, and the man himself was wearing a bright red Santa hat, and Henry wondered what could drive a person to do this kind of thing—to play

a saxophone on a street corner accompanied by a boom box, two days before Christmas. Love of music? Extreme poverty? Rampant exhibitionism? The guy was doing a jazz riff on "Silent Night," which was, frankly, terrible, and Henry wondered if whoever wrote "Silent Night" would have been appalled, and he wondered if maybe it was Irving Berlin, because Irving Berlin wrote "White Christmas" and "Easter Parade," and Sammy Cahn wrote "Chestnuts Roasting on an Open Fire"—oh wait, no, that was Mel Tormé—was he Jewish, too? It's funny how many Jews wrote Christmas songs, but maybe he was wrong about that, because a lot of carols were traditional, coming from jolly old England. But didn't Charles Dickens invent Christmas? That's what he learned somewhere, probably in graduate school when they were deconstructing everything. But the Yule log, that was very old. Pagan. Actually the whole Christmas thing was kind of pagan and that's why everyone liked it. Denise's tattoos. Her fingers. What would it be like to be pagan? You see spirits inhabiting trees and rivers and clouds and feel the whole world is alive with meaning. Terrifying, that's what. Ghosts and goblins! But wouldn't it be marvelous? Marvelous in the true sense of the word—in the sense of miracle, in the sense of awe. Now the sax player moved on to "Have Yourself a Merry Little Christmas," but this time, in spite

of his utter lack of talent, what came out of the horn shimmered with sweet melancholy and Henry felt tears well up his eyes, because, after all, he did love Christmas, and . . . and . . . if only he had had children, it would have been perfect—if only Margaret had wanted them . . . and fuck, Mel Tormé *was* Jewish. . . .

"What are you doing, now?"

He was startled again because it was Daisy again.

"I thought you were going home," he said to her.

"Nah. What are you doing?"

"Just standing here."

"Why?"

"Nobody ever stops to watch these guys play," he explained, "so I thought I would."

"That's so *you*," she said.

His heart began to pound, though he wasn't sure if it was in a good way or a bad way.

"Let's go get some coffee," she suggested.

"I don't know—I have to go shopping."

"There's got to be coffee around here," she went on. "There's a Starbucks up by the Sutter-Stockton, isn't there?"

"I think so," he said. "But I—"

"I know!" she exclaimed. "Let's go to Café Claude!"

"We can't just get coffee there," he said. "It's lunch-time."

"Have you had lunch?"

"No, I guess not."

She smiled and took his hand. "Well, then, come on."

"At least let me give this guy something," he said, and he threw a couple of bucks in the sax case. The musician nodded without skipping a note and Daisy squeezed Henry's hand.

"I love how you do things," she said.

It was only a little bit of a walk to Café Claude, five minutes, maybe even only three, but decidedly in the opposite direction of Macy's. They backtracked along Grant and then down Sutter to tiny Claude Lane and then down the lane all the way to the other end, at Bush Street. That little bottle of Chanel seemed to grow ever more distant.

"Let's sit inside," she said, even though most everyone liked to sit outside under the russet-colored tent because it felt so much like Paris, only foggy. But on a day such as this, the sky cloudless and blue and the sun warming your skin so much you had to take off your jacket, everyone wanted to eat on the terrace. But Daisy knew that Henry believed these happy patrons were dining on their own graves—the cloudless blue was a sign of drought, that's all. He'd be obsessing about all the parched lawns and starving deer and stranded salmon and he wouldn't enjoy his lunch.

So she led him up the stairs to the dining room and, once inside, all the way to the back, as far away from the blue sky as possible. They settled into the last table and in this cave-like corner he finally began to relax. He even leaned toward her until the space between them was compressed into a few tentative inches. How long had it been since he'd been so close to those amazing lips, that adorable nose, those vivid, sparkling eyes? He soon retreated, though, aware that the scent of her hair and wind of her breath were like honey to him.

"You always liked this table," she said.

It's true, he had.

He decided not to speak. He wanted her to say what it was she had come back from the garage to say.

But of course she did no such thing. Instead, she called to the waiter and ordered a glass of rosé. He knew this was his cue to order a glass of Pouilly-Fumé. She always ordered the rosé. He always ordered the Pouilly-Fumé. Surely she sensed the hesitation in him, but she just sat there smiling, her face an open book.

"The Pouilly-Fumé," he finally told the waiter.

"And *pommes frites*!" she cried.

"*Oui*, madam."

"To nibble on while we decide."

Because that is also what they always did.

The waiter disappeared, and Daisy folded her hands in front of her. She looked at Henry as if she were contemplating a great work of art.

"Okay, Daisy," he said, giving up. "What's going on?"

"Why should anything be going on?"

"Please."

"Oh, I don't know," she replied. "It's just that when I saw you, I couldn't stop myself."

"Stop yourself from what?"

She lowered her eyes. He wondered why women do that—lower their eyes. He knew there were these universal facial expressions—for instance, when you meet someone with whom you are acquainted, your eyebrows go up—it's a way of saying you intend no violence—every single person in the world does it, regardless of culture—but what about lowering your eyes? Do guys lower their eyes? Does he? People in China don't smile for no reason like we do. We're always smiling. It certainly doesn't mean we're happy. It just means we're morons. Emotion is so hard to pin down! He wondered what emotion his own face was conveying and what Daisy was intuiting from the curve of his mouth or the arch of his eyebrow, but he knew that even if he had had a mirror, he himself would not have been able to discern what his feelings were. He never looked natural in a mirror. It was like in quantum physics: observing the object alters it. So you can never see yourself as you are. Actually, when he looked in the mirror, the impression of his own unreality made him kind of nauseous.

Unless he was combing his hair. Because your hair is somehow apart from you, an accoutrement, an add-on, like a lampshade.

"What are you thinking about?" she asked.

"You," he said.

"What about me?"

"Everything," he said.

The waiter came with the french fries and also set the wineglasses down before them. They ordered their lunches, and when the waiter left, they lifted their glasses, hers sparkling pink, his pale straw—

"To our time together," she said, clinking his glass.

He took a sip of wine and nibbled on a couple of potatoes.

"So, your divorce is final now?" he asked.

"Oh my God, yes, for a long time."

"How long?"

"Two years."

"That's not all that long, Daisy. How did the kids take it?"

"They're fine. Well, Denny was very angry for a while, but Tasha was too young to fully understand. She just accepted. Then Denny did, too. I mean they hardly saw their father when we were married, so it wasn't that big of a change for them. Honestly, he sees the kids more now than before. He's on a mission to prove he's the world's best dad. You never had any kids?"

"No, as I said—"

"It's a shame. You really would be the world's best dad."

"I doubt that."

"I don't."

Again they fell into silence.

"I don't know why I broke up with you," she said.

"I do."

"Then tell me."

"Because we were married to other people, and it was wrong, and I was a jerk," he explained.

"You weren't a jerk."

"I was. I didn't care about who we hurt. Your kids, our spouses. I was a selfish jerk."

"I don't think that's why I broke it off."

"Yeah, it was."

"No. I think it was because I was afraid."

"That's what I'm saying. You were afraid of hurting your family."

"No. I was afraid of what you required of me. You wanted me to give myself to you. To actually be there. To fight things through with you. You were a very demanding lover. I mean that in a good way."

"I was a jerk," he repeated. "I'm a smotherer. Though not with Margaret, as it turns out. I don't demand anything of her."

"That's because you don't love her."

He was relieved when the food arrived and he could comment on his fish and ask her about her pasta. But what she had just said—that he didn't love Margaret. Of course he loved her. Why would he have stuck it out if he didn't love her? Maybe it wasn't the same as what he'd felt for Daisy, but was that love? Wasn't that just the excitement of an affair? The forbidden fruit? I mean, look at her. So fucking sexy. With those red curls and freckles and—

"So your pasta is good?" he said.

"You already asked me that."

He stared down at his trout. Much better: it wasn't the least bit sexy. It was fish.

In fact, at this moment he loved his trout. When he looked at the trout his groin did not tingle. When he looked at the trout he did not doubt himself or question his past or imagine some alternate future. Though he did wonder about what happened to the trout before it reached this plate. Part of him hoped it had traveled far and wide through foamy white-water streams, but he knew it most likely had had a bitter life in an overcrowded fish farm. And now it sat there on a white plate on a white tablecloth in a white sauce ready to be eaten by a white man. Actually the white cloth was covered with a sheet of white paper, so it really wasn't a white-tablecloth restaurant. It was just a white-paper restaurant. White is also the color of death, he remembered. Poor fish! Although he had to admit it looked delicious. There were bits of wild mushrooms floating about, too, and that gave the whole thing an inviting frisson of danger, because mushrooms—wild mushrooms—all those people mistaking death cap for caesarea. Italians mostly. That's why he always stuck with boletus and chanterelle. Can't mistake those. They were everywhere just now, including in his trout, though chanterelles mostly come up in January and February, at least out at Lake Lagunitas where he liked to hunt for them, but these days you could find the most exotic things in the grocery store, mostly from Oregon, because, well we have no goddamned rain in California, and so he thought about the drought once again, and the people eating outside and . . . *Mind!* he screamed (internally, not out

loud, thank God), *Mind! Shut up! Shut up! Shut up!* Because
for once he wanted to concentrate on the here and now. Yes.
He admitted it: he *wanted* to concentrate on Daisy—yes,
Daisy—yes, be here with Daisy—yes, find out what the hell
they were doing together—yes, he wanted to—he wanted—
he didn't know what! And in that moment he realized that
he hadn't always been this way—that his mind hadn't always
wandered quite so much—not that he hadn't always loved
to cogitate on the things he saw during the day or on ideas
that had come to him by chance or that his inner voice hadn't
always been loquacious, to say the least, but this constant
monologue, this incessant vocalizing of every moronic scin-
tilla of thought, this had grown into a kind of compulsion in
the last two or three years. And with a terrible start he realized: only since Daisy. It started when he lost Daisy and went
back to Margaret. What could that mean?

He raised his eyes from the whiteness of the tablecloth
and the fish and the sauce, and he said to Daisy, "Why did
you divorce Edward?"

She laughed. "You are an idiot. Because of you."

"Because of me? Why?"

"Because I saw what a relationship was supposed to be.
I understood what it felt to actually love someone and to be
loved by someone. I couldn't settle anymore."

"But, Daisy, it was so short. We slept together what? Once? Twice? We knew it was wrong."

"What difference does it make how many times? Eighteen, actually."

"But was it ever a real relationship?"

"You tell me."

He truly did not know the answer to this question, so he said, "And that was that with Edward?"

"That was that."

"That's crazy," he said. "First you break it off with me, and then you get divorced because of me? And then you take up with some guy you say was horrible?"

"Why did you stay with Margaret?" she shot back.

"Because I'm married to her. Marriage is supposed to mean something."

"But you don't love her."

"You don't know that."

"I do know that," she insisted.

"Why do you think I don't love her?" he asked.

"And you think she loves you?"

"Yes. Of course."

She set down her fork and grasped the edge of the table. "Look me in the eye, Henry, and tell me: Do you love Margaret?"

"Yes," he declared. "I love her."

"Then I guess we don't have anything more to talk about."

"Why not?"

She pushed her chair from the table, scrambled into her coat, her fur hat, her gloves.

"I don't know what I was thinking," she said.

"I don't understand you . . ."

"Bones, I apologize. I shouldn't have done this. All I know is, I haven't stopped thinking about you a single day in the last four years. I fucking dream about you. It's stupid and it's crazy and I'm sorry."

And with that, she fled Café Claude.

———

A few of the diners looked up, the waiter hung near the bar trying to gauge whether to bring the check, and then all went back to normal. But Henry Quantum was still shivering in the frigid wind of her departure. He took several deep breaths to calm himself, as he had learned in his one session at the Green Gulch Zen Center and then at the retreat he had attended at Spirit Rock, and shut his eyes so he could realign his chakras but mostly so he wouldn't have to look at the seat she had just vacated. What just happened? he asked himself. What had she said? What had he said? Only half opening his eyes, he motioned to the waiter, asked him to remove her plate of pasta.

"Is the light bothering you?" the waiter asked.

"Something's in my eye," he said.

He decided to finish his fish. The fish that had taken that long journey from the fish farm to this plate. He would not waste its life. As his has been wasted. Have I really wasted my life? he wondered. I'm forty. Past fucking forty by three fucking months.

He took another bite. It tasted like dust. Not really. It tasted like fish. But he heard his inner voice say it tasted like dust. Jesus! Why be so dramatic? You had an affair. You blew it. Just eat your fish.

You're married, for Christ's sake.

And this reminded him about the perfume.

He asked for the check, left an overgenerous tip, and stepped out onto Claude Lane.

"Perfume!" he declared to no one in particular. "Perfume!"

And so he resumed his route toward Macy's, but in spite of his new resolve, found himself walking at a snail's pace, his arms folded in thought.

CHAPTER 5

2:24–4:16 p.m.

Of all the people to run into on this very day—in the midst of his critical mission to buy perfume for his Margaret— why on earth did it have to be Daisy? Why couldn't it be— he couldn't think of anyone except for Donald Trump for some reason. But even Donald Trump would have been bet- ter than Daisy.

And why vision science? That's what she said she was studying, right? *How we see.* How can you see how we see? Just because you determine some neuron shoots off at a cer- tain wavelength, what does that tell you about *seeing*? Still, it was great she was in school. She'd actually end up with the PhD he'd never gotten. But what did she mean, she never stopped dreaming about him? She'd been living with some other guy: the one he once got a glimpse of in the white suit and the Panama hat at that fundraiser they both happened to attend a year or so after they'd stopped seeing each other. Seeing each other. Did they in fact see each other? Yes, perhaps they had. Perhaps that's what she meant. She had been seen. That's what scared her and that's what she wanted back. But you can't have things back. It's like going on the same vacation twice. It's never the same.

He meandered back to where he had first run into Daisy, in front of SlinkyBlink, and here at last he stopped and took a breath. In the window were shredded jeans and rhinestone-studded T-shirts, flouncy skirts, platform shoes, bright-colored handbags with huge buckles—things he could barely imagine anyone wearing, except maybe Denise, the art director, and Gladys, the receptionist, but not really—Gladys was ultraconservative in her dress because she wanted to be taken seriously and become a copywriter. And he was pretty sure Denise was more Goth than SlinkyBlink, if people were still called Goth, which Henry seriously doubted. This all got back to the question of *seeing*. Fashion looked great one year and stupid the next. But the clothes—they stayed just the same. How is it they no longer looked the same? How is it the woman you loved last year is no longer the woman you love this year? And to whom was he referring? Daisy or Margaret?

But Daisy said she dreamed about him every day.

When he thought about it, it was all crazy. Before the divorce, Daisy had it all. The mansion in Ross, the rich and beautiful husband, the two brilliant kids, the garden parties, the Tesla runabout, the Land Rover, the Lynch-Bages as the house wine ($200 a pop!), and the Dom Pérignon in the fridge. Why did she throw that all away?

She'd asked him, "Did you ever write that novel?" He had forgotten that he even wanted to write a book, that he'd actually taken notes, sketched out a few scenes, did a little research. Where was all that stuff? He knew very well where it was. In the earthen storeroom in the back of the garage, in a box, with the mildew and the smell of mouse turds and mushrooms. Maybe he should take it out and try again. But no. That would be Daisy entering his life again, too. That's what she did to him. False hope, he called it. He had zero talent and he knew it.

True, he had written little stories and poems for her. "I love your writing!" she'd say, her face flushed, tears forming in her eyes. He didn't believe her, but he swelled with pride anyway. Even now he could feel her enthusiasm course through him. She would be spread out on the couch with his typed sheets piled next to her and would throw open her arms as if he had just written *Moby Dick* or *Love Story* or something, and would swallow him up. He figured it was just the pleasure she felt for having been the object of all this writing. She would shower him with kisses, wrap her legs around him, and seem to melt beneath him. But perhaps he had not really understood these moments. Perhaps her passion was much deeper than that. Maybe it wasn't just flattery when she gushed that no one had ever written her poetry before, not to mention the little love stories. Maybe it was more. Maybe he was a good writer, after all.

This whole business of writing was now in his mind, and his struggle with it. In graduate school he found he could compose a decent paper, but Daisy had liberated something else in him. For her, he conjured medieval lovers, stolen hours, secret trysts, island hideaways, and erotic messages conveyed by carrier pigeon. Ordinary joes and janes were transformed by ecstasy or condemned to fathomless depths of despair. The sex in these tales was never explicit, mainly because it embarrassed him to write about it, but it didn't seem to matter. Daisy wrote those parts in her own imagination, and the real-life lovemaking was immediate and overwhelming and, he had to admit, wilder than anything he could have captured on paper.

Why had he insisted he loved Margaret?

But he knew he must not call Daisy, must not start all

that again. It was so much easier, so much cleaner is how he put it to himself, to live a life without secrets. Secrets cause pain, and the avoidance of pain was his current preoccupation. So he moved away from the display window at SlinkyBlink—these places come and go so fast, he told himself—like everything else, like everything else—and continued on his way to Macy's, although this time he did decide to go by way of Sutter and not Geary, because he didn't want to pass the saxophonist again. Or —he stopped himself just as his foot touched the sidewalk on the other side of the street—maybe it really was because he was hoping to run into Daisy again, knowing she parked at the Sutter-Stockton garage and this was the direction she would have to take to get there, and perhaps she was dawdling, maybe even waiting for him beside the flower shop near the garage entrance. The flower shop run by the beautiful East European blonde—Henry guessed she was Serbian by the crisp line of her chin and the way she had of dispensing with anyone who gave her a hard time—but she certainly was a great beauty, and he wondered why such a beauty would work in a flower shop— well, probably because she owned it, she and that husband of hers, who was quite a bit older and had the head of a buffalo—couldn't she have done better? Couldn't she have married a rich man or been a fashion

model or something? He admired her, actually. For not trying to get by on her looks. Because, let's face it, if you're
extremely good-looking, you get much further. There was
a Darwinian force at work there. Surely there were studies
on this. He would look into it when he got back to the office.

Henry trudged up the Sutter Street hill, and when he
reached the entrance to the garage, he did look in, and the
beautiful Serbian woman was indeed sitting on her stool in
the flower shop, clipping roses, but Daisy was nowhere to be
seen. *How do you know you're in Serbia?* he quipped to himself. *When you can choose between several war criminals in the
presidential election.* He read that online and for some reason it
stuck with him. And here she was cutting flowers, one of the
most beautiful women in San Francisco. And what about the
Jews and Palestinians? And Islamic State and Al Qaeda and
that horrible business in Paris with the newspaper and then the
theater, and those morons in Somalia or Nigeria or wherever
that Boko-whatever was. And then Russia going into Ukraine
and China in Tibet and North Korea with that new guy, and
then Iran and—it could be World War III at any second. We
don't think about it. We go on as if everything is fine. But a
bomb, a nuclear one, why not? Everyone in the world is afraid
of something. The Serbs are afraid of the Muslims because
they're afraid all Muslims want to go back to the Dark Ages

and if you don't believe what they believe, then they want to kill you. Actually, he was afraid of the Muslims, too, he was sorry to admit. Like on the plane. You try to be cool about it, but let's face it. Then again, when you think about it, guess what? They're afraid, too. Afraid of their children becoming polluted by the rest of us. Afraid of being taken over because they were already taken over. Afraid of being profiled and abused by . . . people like me!

And here it was Christmas!

Jesus is about love and forgiveness and joy and brotherhood, isn't he? Not that Henry believed in Jesus. Not really. Only when he was scared, maybe. Or when he was really, really alone. Maybe it was because he *wanted* to believe in Jesus. Like he did when he was a kid. You know, beginner's mind. That's what he was after. Beginner's mind. He was ashamed to say he mostly prayed to Jesus when he couldn't sleep or if he thought someone was breaking into the house, which was frequently. As if God cared if Henry Quantum had insomnia or someone was sneaking into his house. Jesus has to be realistic, too, he scolded himself.

And yet—if God didn't care, if God didn't care about Henry Quantum, if God didn't care about each and every one of his creatures individually, if he didn't have the power to care for every single soul at the same time, then he wasn't

God, was he? The mystical Jews, the cabalists, they thought that God had retreated from the world because the world was too broken for him, or maybe the world was broken because he retreated, Henry couldn't quite remember. But it was true. The world was broken. Broken, broken, broken. That's the God's truth.

He stood on the corner of Stockton and Sutter with JoS. A. Bank behind him and the new CVS across to his right, and Henry Quantum was bereft of God, although the Starbucks across the street did seem to be graced with people coming in thirsty and going out holding their paper cups of coffee, and all the money going into those registers, and all the people typing away on their laptops listening to something on their earbuds. And that made him feel a little better.

Maybe she's in Starbucks, he thought.

He crossed Sutter but hesitated to go inside. Instead, he peered through the big plate glass windows and scanned the tables. Sadly, no Daisy.

"Perfume!" he said. "Perfume!"

So he continued his way down Stockton toward Geary, past the Campton Place Hotel, which was now the Taj Campton Place spelled in garish gold letters on the awning, and this saddened him, because why does everything change? Why can't you hold on to anything? Why? Ask Buddha! He'll tell you! Holding on is the source of pain. And pain is what we don't want. He'd been studying Buddhism lately. And here it was Indians who owned the Taj, teaching him this all over again. Though he preferred Zen, and that was Japanese.

Come to think of it, Zen didn't say very much about pain. It was more about the immediacy of experience, about nothingness and everythingness being sort of one and the same, and also he was very taken with this idea they called lightning Zen, where you could achieve enlightenment by putting your shoes on your head. He'd actually tried it. Margaret came into the bedroom and turned around and walked out.

He also liked reading those Zen koans. His favorite was:

Lightning flashes,
Sparks shower.
In one blink of your eyes,
You have missed seeing.

And there it all came round again. Daisy studying the eye. Him trying to see what she was up to. But that's the problem, the whole quantum, Zen, Heisenberg problem: If you look, you miss seeing. If you don't look, there's no way you can see, either.

He had been inching down Stockton, thinking, Only through action can one achieve enlightenment, but all action is useless. And since all action is useless, he stood stock-still. You put one foot in front of the other in order to get somewhere, but all you get is nowhere. It was like Zeno's paradox, only for the soul.

That's when he noticed the woman.

The woman with the three children.

They were in front of the Nike store having a meltdown. Actually it was the mother who was having the meltdown and the kids were staring at her with stricken faces and probably wet pants. She screamed at the top of her lungs and stomped her feet.

What an interesting family! he thought. Why? Because the mom was white, the eldest daughter was black, the little boy was Chinese, and the two-year-old looked kind of Latina. That's America. Naturally, they didn't get along.

"If you cry one more time—if you ask for one more soda or ice cream—if you hit one another even a little, if you whine, complain, run off, or beg for one more thing, or," she said screaming, "if you say anything at all—then, then—that's *it!*"

The two older kids became quiet as stones, but the baby,

the Latina one, or maybe it was Latino, who can tell at that age?—started howling more loudly than ever.

"Goddammit! Goddammit!" the woman yelled.

"It's okay, Mom," said the middle child, taking her hand. "We'll take care of it."

And the older girl reached into the stroller and started cooing and tickling. "See?"

Oh, how Henry's heart went out to those children and to their mother. He knew exactly what she was feeling! She can't take it anymore. She's had it. That's it.

But no matter what the little girl did, the baby wouldn't stop crying. The mother half collapsed against the plate glass windows of the Nike store and began to sob. And Henry thought to himself, here she is, the woman who got her wish. She'd wanted those children, she'd dreamt of them, even had their names picked out long before she knew what they might look like, or even what country they might come from; she'd convinced her husband she had to have at least three, when he would have been happy with one; she'd explored and researched fifteen different agencies, interviewed dozens of adoptive parents, hired a whole office full of lawyers, and coughed up twenty, thirty, maybe fifty grand for each one of those kids, even though they couldn't possibly afford it—and finally her dream came true: she traveled to far-off lands—three different continents in five years—to rescue each one of these children from their shoddy orphanages and corrupt caretakers; she triumphed as she disembarked the aircraft at SFO, presenting her new baby conquests to their new grandparents, uncles, and aunts; and then diligently she fed and clothed them, lavished them with toys and books, televisions and computers, Xboxes and Wiis, reporting it all daily on Facebook and Twitter and Pinterest—and for what? So that she might see, in this one prescient moment, that her life was no longer her own, that it had become a shambles, a nightmare; that the kids couldn't care less what she had gone through to get them, that they were spoiled rotten and that she hated them, hated them profoundly, and wanted nothing more than to run back to Nordstrom this very second, run back *alone*—as if they never existed, as if she could unwind the coil she'd wrapped around her own neck and be free.

But of course that's not what happened. Instead, she gently touched her eldest daughter on the shoulder and took up the baby from the stroller and said, "Ha-ha-ha, goo-goo-goo," gently slipped a bottle in her mouth, and gathered the other two around her. They formed a kind of phalanx of family with the stroller in the middle, and calmly recommenced their walk up the street. Henry could not take his eyes off them, that United Nations of children loping along beside their mother in such careful quietude; and she, as if nothing at all had happened, cooing at the baby and instructing her children to stop at the corner and wait for the light.

Margaret had not wanted kids. Perhaps she had once, but something in her changed, and then she didn't anymore. Probably she was worried that children would derail her career, ruin her figure. She was a big real estate developer now. But he, Henry, had longed for them, and witnessing the agony of this desperate mother had not caused him to sympathize with Margaret one bit, because in the simple gesture of the middle child taking his mother's hand, and in the way the eldest girl tried her best to stop the baby's crying, he understood he was witnessing the emancipating power of a child's love.

Was it too late for them to have kids? Margaret was forty-two. You can still have kids when you're forty-two, can't you? And anyway, they could always adopt. In his mind's eye it was Christmas morning, and scampering down the stairs at first light, rounding the tree on a beeline to the pile of presents, they would come, his children, and one by one they would tear open their gifts, while they— was it Margaret in this picture, he couldn't quite tell—sat with their mugs of coffee watching, with hearts overflowing, the joyous tumult. They would have three, just like that woman, only it would be two boys and a girl, and the eldest boy would be the protector of the other two, and his name would be Hunter because that was the name Henry had always wanted for himself. Hunter had sandy hair and could already throw a football at the age of six, and Charlotte, whom everyone called Charlie, was five, with wild, red curls—which made him pretty sure the woman seated beside him wasn't Margaret—but he let that slide because little Charlie loved to sing and dance and now she twirled herself over to Henry and jumped on his lap and kissed him and said, "Oh, dear Papa! What a happy home!" As for the youngest one, the three-year-old—well, he would be named Dylan and he was towheaded and had beautiful pink cheeks and was completely content with his hand-painted wooden train—little did he know that in the closet was his very first tricycle. And from the kitchen the aroma of gingerbread and French toast, and on the stereo Bach or Handel, and the doorbell would ring and the carolers would be out on the front lawn knee-deep in snow . . .

But then it went blank, because someone had bumped into him.

"Oh, oh, I'm so sorry!" she said.

And he replied, "No, no, it's my fault."

And she said, "Yeah, maybe it is. You're sort of standing right in the middle of the sidewalk."

And that was his cue to continue on his way down Stockton toward Macy's.

———

He didn't have to walk far before he noticed the human robot at the entrance to Union Square. The human robot had painted himself silver from head to toe—clothes, skin, shoes, and bowler hat—and was currently frozen like a statue, as no one had put any money into his soup can, which was also painted silver. Even though Henry had ignored this guy a million times, today he found himself crossing the plaza to observe him. He wanted to see him move like a machine. But the human robot remained motionless, not a robot but a human statue, or maybe a robot that hadn't been plugged in. But that turned out to be far more amazing than Henry had imagined. The guy didn't bat an eye, twitch a finger, and you couldn't even see him breathe. Who could do that? How could he so completely quiet the teeming multitude of himself? Henry knew he had only to drop a dollar or two into the soup can and the statue would move like a mechanical being, which, of course, was his whole shtick, but Henry suddenly decided he wanted to see how long he could keep up this statue business even though his right arm was out-stretched as if to shake your hand and the other was twisted in a weird left-handed salute, and his eyes were frozen open and his lips were curled into a rigid smile. He wondered for a minute if the guy really was made of metal. There was not one iota of movement.

And then with a laugh Henry Quantum realized that he himself hadn't moved a muscle, either; he had been uncon-sciously mimicking the robot man for the last two minutes. Now, that was lightning Zen! But, of course, as soon as Henry became aware of it, he lost it—like the Heisenberg thing again. But the robot man—the robot man had learned somehow to forget his stillness, to become unaware of it, to lose himself on some other plane of existence, perhaps by focusing those unblinking eyes on some distant object. And that's when the subject of the Sombrero Galaxy returned to Henry's consciousness. Because it seemed to him that the vastness of the universe was no different that the vastness of this man's soul, and the impossibility of understanding either of them oppressed him so much that he cried out, "Do something, for God's sake!" And everyone thought he was yelling at robo-man, but Henry knew otherwise.

Someone next to him explained, "You have to give him money."

"Yeah, I know," replied Henry.

"Eventually, though, he'll have to move even without the money."

"I have a feeling they can last like this for a couple of hours," Henry said, remembering something he had read. "Here, I'll give him five bucks."

"No, don't," said the man. "He should make some gesture to show he cares about us."

"But the whole point is for us to give him money."

"No, he should care about his audience. He should want to connect with us. And since he can hear every word we're saying, he'll definitely hold out till we pay him."

"I don't mind paying him," Henry said.

The man asked, "Where are you from?"

"From here."

"Figures. But it's kind of cool that you still take the time to watch these guys. We're from Oklahoma City." The man indicated his family with a sweep of his hand. "You would think he would do something for my kids," he said. But the fact of the matter was the kids weren't interested. They were playing on their phones. "They might as well have stayed in Oklahoma," their father remarked.

"Maybe if we get him to perform, they'll pay attention," Henry suggested, because by now he was feeling responsible for the robo-man's well-being, and this guy from Oklahoma City sort of frightened him.

"No, no, don't. Believe me, he'll break. How long can he keep this up?"

"I don't know. A long time."

"Everyone has a breaking point, my friend."

"I guess people are pretty tough in Oklahoma City," Henry remarked.

"You ever been to Oklahoma City?"

"No. I've never been to Oklahoma City. All I know about it is cows or something."

"That's Kansas City."

"Oh, right, right. You guys are the bombing."

"For God's sake."

"No, I mean—jeez, I'm sorry—"

"We're much more than that."

"Of course you are. Restaurants, theater, opera."

"Opera?"

"Steaks?"

"You people think San Francisco is the be-all and end-all and the rest of the country is filled with hayseeds and sheep fuckers."

"I didn't say that."

"All you've got is queers and Chinese."

Henry wanted to leave, but he felt if he fled now, he'd be capitulating to this guy's bullying. So they stayed side by side, watching the robot man do nothing. Henry felt terrible. Why did he have to bring up that whole bombing thing? And opera? And *steaks*? Okay, the guy was a bigoted asshole, but hadn't they shared something? A bit of human interaction, a moment of intellectual exchange, of artistic appreciation?

"We do have more than queers and Chinese," Henry said. "We also have Japanese. And quite a few Russians."

The guy turned to him with a bemused expression.

"What are you," he replied, "stupid?"

Henry reached into his pocket, found five bucks, threw it into the silver-painted soup can, and bolted up the stairs to the plaza. Out of the corner of his eye he could see robot man spring to life. That's how wars are started! he thought. Someone blurts out a hurtful word and even though he didn't mean anything by it the other guy says something back and before you know it, nuclear winter! It brought to mind *War and Peace* and Levin having his epiphanies that vanished in the light of morning, and the vast armies moving about like chess pieces for the generals, but on the field of battle, a tangle of discord and confusion and dumb luck and grotesque misfortune—not to mention Pierre! Because no one really controls anything, do they? Not when they're in the middle of it. You may think you have a handle on something, like history, but you don't, you can't. It's just a trick of perspective, a fun-house mirror, some version of the world that has nothing to do with reality, because none of us know what is happening to us, ever. Oh, wait. Levin was in *Anna Karenina.*

Henry could not resist the urge to glance back, like Lot's wife, only it was the guy from Oklahoma who was the pillar of salt, frozen with anger, although Henry hoped he was just mesmerized by the performance of the human robot. The kids were still on their smartphones.

But now atop the plaza, Henry was confronted by something he hadn't expected. It wasn't the huge Christmas tree—you could see that a block away—or even the giant Hanukkah menorah on the east end of Union Square, no, it was the ice-skating rink that had been set up where the stage usually was, and people were gliding round the tiny rink as if in some New Hampshire wood. They wore mittens and floppy-eared woolen caps even though it was sixty-five degrees out. A huge crowd had lined up between a set of ropes, anxiously awaiting their turns, unconcerned that a large hand-painted sign declared they were allowed on the ice for only half an hour at a time. The children could barely

contain their excitement, and the parents, in spite of trying
their best to contain them, sooner or later succumbed to the
same anticipation. Christmas music blared from the loud-
speakers and off to one side Emporio Rulli café was selling
hot chocolate and espressos. It was all a strange cartoon version of Rockefeller Center, with red and green bunting and
mounds of cotton snow and Santa's bejeweled sleigh parked
on the roof of the hut where you rented your skates. But
for all its ersatz atmospherics, it was also a genuinely happy
scene, and it got Henry to wondering: What is it that makes
us happy, after all? A person imitates a statue, a refriger-
ated concrete slab imitates a winter wonderland—and we're
filled with joy. He remembered when Margaret went to EST,
or whatever they were calling it then, the Forum or Land-
mark or something, and all she talked about was "authenticity." Maybe it helped her, but he doubted very highly
whether she, or anyone else, could be *authentically* authentic. You know what Sartre called authenticity? Resisting
the pressures of the external world. But if you lived in the
external world, you would always be in relationship to it,
so how could you ever be authentic in a world of culture?
He thought again about his Papua New Guinea idea—saw
in his mind's eye the bare-breasted women and the mostly
naked men. Ahhh, he sighed. But they stick animal bones

through their lower lips, don't they? That would be uncomfortable. And the women get old and ugly really fast, with breasts like two hanging frying pans and bumpy nipples the size of studded snow tires.

And they eat sago! What the hell is sago anyway? He'd read enough to know it was poisonous until you processed it, and what if you processed it wrong? But what did it taste like anyway? It was a mystery. And also crickets. They eat crickets and grubs. Although maybe he could manage the occasional monkey. But then it occurred to him: this is also culture. It was useless to go to Papua New Guinea! No authenticity there, either. So how can anyone be himself? Can anyone even *be*? Is there really a me? And if there's no me, how can I ever be *free*?

He was still thinking about Sartre—whom he had not read since college, and then only skimmingly—but it seemed to him Sartre said the idea of freedom was so terrifying and boundless that it made you nauseous. And he did feel a little sick actually.

In the meantime, though, he continued to watch the ice skaters make their little circles around the tiny rink and beyond them the hawkers of souvenirs and the bums looking for handouts and the street jugglers putting on a show up and down the ticket line, and, farther off, an enclave of

Rastafarians banging steel drums and some guy strumming a guitar and singing Bob Dylan songs, and beyond that was Geary Street with its Christmas traffic and its sidewalks thick with pedestrians, and beyond that, directly behind the pedestrians, in fact, every window decked with golden wreaths and silvery lights, was Macy's.

The nausea got a little worse, so he found a vacant bench and sat himself down. He checked his watch. It was already past three. He had read about a physics experiment in which they had made time disappear, at least as far as the observer was concerned. They make a time hole by speeding up the speed of light going into an event and slowing it down coming out, or maybe it was vice versa, but whatever, and the event just disappears as if it never happened. Even though it did. Right before your eyes. Of course they did this on a micro scale of like a forty-trillionth of a second—but for that forty-trillionth of a second, time ceased to be. He checked his watch again. He should have been back at the office two hours ago. But it was nearly Christmas! Why should he even think about work this time of year? And anyway, there was the office party tomorrow, and then everyone would be off for three days, and then the no-man's-land between Christmas and New Year's Eve, when nothing gets done and most everyone just goes skiing or flies off to Maui. We make our own time holes, but, oh, if only time could really disappear!

He looked up from his revelry. Macy's loomed over him, over the whole square, a great shadow.

I could get the perfume anywhere, he said to himself. There was Neiman catty-cornered cross the street. On the other side of the square was Saks. Or that little perfumery run by that old French couple just a block or so away. He could even buy it online with overnight delivery. Why am I so stuck on Macy's? he asked himself.

It was a huge structure taking up an entire city block. And even that wasn't the whole thing. The men's store was a separate building on the other side of Stockton Street. Macy's was so big it was beyond comprehension.

If only he hadn't run into Daisy!

How could you not love Daisy? Anyone could see how great she was. It wasn't just that she was smart—Margaret was also smart. Or that she was beautiful and funny and adventurous in bed. What set Daisy apart, he now understood, was that she had heart. And she experienced in her being the fact that other people had hearts, too. That Henry Quantum had a heart, even though he thought maybe he didn't.

But he told her he loved Margaret. So why was the Chanel No. 5 weighing on him like a slab of granite? Perfume is a last-minute gift, and he knew it, a gift that required no thought, and it would be accepted as such—a pathetic, self-serving gesture of appeasement. And while it was true no one else could buy Margaret perfume—only a husband or a lover can buy a woman perfume—still, it was as impersonal as a cashier's check. If the buying of perfume had been a ritual between them, if, for instance, at every Christmas he presented her with her favorite scent and a loving card, a marking of the time they shared together, that would be one thing—but let's face it, he hardly ever bought her perfume, or anything else for that matter. He used to. But he reminded himself again that she never really liked what he bought. And these days, he rarely had the urge to please her. And why was that? Maybe Margaret wasn't the kindest person in the world, not like Daisy, but she was very good-looking and could be wickedly funny, and once upon a time she, too, had been adventurous in bed. And wasn't Margaret a good partner and easy to talk to? And didn't she put up with his foibles, which he knew were manifold? And they shared the household chores without rancor, and there was some kind of tenderness between them, wasn't there?

So Henry had to ask himself: What is the truth of this perfume?

And even if there was no such thing as an authentic act, on this day, sitting on this bench, Henry wanted to know, wanted to know truly, what it was he wanted to do and who it was he had become, and who it was he wanted to be.

And that is when Santa Claus sat down beside him.

The thing is, it wasn't exactly Santa—no red suit, no black boots, no floppy cap—it was just an ordinary guy with a thick white beard and a huge, round tummy. His long ashen hair had been pulled back into a thin ponytail, and he wore suspenders over a pale blue short-sleeve shirt because he was too hot even in winter, and his trousers were charcoal gray and his shoes had thick crepe soles— and when Henry stared at him, the guy said, "Yeah, I know. All year long I'm just a fat guy with a beard, but in December, suddenly I'm Santa. Especially now, with just two days to go. I don't mind. The kids come up to me and I ask them if they've been good, and the mothers aren't even afraid of me like they are the rest of the year. But this isn't *Miracle on Thirty-Fourth Street* and I'm not the real Santa Claus."

"I guess I was staring," said Henry.

"It's fine. Sometimes I get off on it. I'm just having a tough day. Sometimes even Santa has a shitty day."

"I've had a strange day myself."

"Yeah, you look a little forlorn, if you don't mind my saying so."

"Forlorn?" said Henry.

"Haggard."

"What are you, an English professor?"

"Cabdriver. But that doesn't mean I'm a moron. Actually I went to Princeton."

"Really?"

"Yeah, all Princeton graduates drive taxis."

"Oh. Sorry."

"It's okay. Bad day for Santa."

"I really look forlorn and haggard?"

"You do. All bent over, holding your head in your hands."

"I didn't realize I was."

"Yeah, you were."

"It's funny—the day started with me thinking about distance and the speed of light—I mean, about how far away from us everything really is, and how it's impossible to ever truly experience anything in the moment, even yourself. There's always the mediation of time, of space, of something that comes between the self and everything else. It kind of depressed me. Sounds crazy, doesn't it?"

"Not at all. You have a philosophical mind."

"You know, the light from the Sombrero Galaxy takes thirty million years to get to us, so when we look at the pictures Hubble takes, we're seeing it as it was thirty million years ago."

"Yeah, I know that."

"So we have no idea what it looks like now, or if it even still exists."

"But it exists for us."

"As a photograph. As an image on our retinas. And the thing is, this morning all I could think about was that terrible, terrible distance. And then I ran into this old friend, this old girlfriend actually, and the same feeling came over me— that distance times time equals impossible, if that makes any sense."

"Yeah, I get you."

"And now I have to decide whether or not to buy my wife some perfume at Macy's."

"I see."

"It sucks," said Henry.

"Well, you know there is another theory out there."

"Of what?"

"That the universe is really two-dimensional, and that space doesn't exist at all. That all of space is just an illusion, and we're, like, holographs."

"That's nuts."

"It's the latest theory."

"Are you also a physicist?"

"Just interested in how the world works."

"Yeah, it'd be great to know how the world works."

"Well, this theory arose from a simple well-known fact. That at the level of quantum, a particle can be at two places at the same time. This has been a great mystery—how can something be in two places at the same time? And the answer they came up with is that there is really no such thing as two places. Because space itself is an illusion. It has to do with black holes and the energy that gets sucked into them and the energy that gets pushed back out and how more energy actually comes out than goes in, or something like that, but the point is, they say that at the edge of a black hole, all the data of all the material that has been sucked into it is encoded on its lip like a residue or a hologram, and therefore is not lost, and that actually our entire universe is nothing but a kind of super massive black hole, and we are simply representations of what's inside it. It's like looking at the hologram on a credit card. We're just data on a flat surface, made three-dimensional by the addition of light."

"So there is no space between us? Between you and me?"

"Not really."

"And no space within us?"

"No."

"Kind of like the Buddhist idea?"

"Kind of."

"And you said a quantum particle can be in two places at one time?"

"Yes, it can."

"Because space is an illusion?"

"I think that's it."

Henry leaned back against the bench. Wow, he thought, I must have been wrong about everything. Maybe it really is possible to connect to another human being on the deepest level. But even more amazing to him was that it was possible to be in two places at one time. This was the breathless revelation he'd been yearning for all day. To be both in love with Margaret and not in love with Margaret, to both desire Daisy with all his heart and avoid Daisy with all his might, to both walk into Macy's and buy that goddamned perfume and to never set foot in Macy's as long as he lived; and what's more, it was also possible to do one's work diligently and put it off indefinitely, to fetch his brother-in-law at the airport and also to let him wait till he turned to dust, and if he really wanted, he could stay on this bench forever talking with this man who was both Santa Claus and not Santa Claus, and at the same time he could fly off to Papua New Guinea and never come back.

He thought about all this and then suddenly and quite unexpectedly, he told everything he was thinking to the man with the white beard.

The older man smiled warmly, stood up, and placed his hand upon Henry's shoulder.

"The only problem," he said, "is that you're not a quantum particle."

"Yeah." Henry sighed. "And you're not Santa."

"But on that," the fat man replied, "you'd be wrong." He leaned back and laughed the best Santa laugh Henry ever heard.

And then Henry was left alone on the bench, Macy's in front of him, the ice rink behind, and the sun above him beginning its drift into the sea.

He looked again across Geary at all the people passing in front of Macy's huge bronze doors—and realized just how far away they were.

PART TWO

MARGARET

CHAPTER 6

December 23rd, 9:15 a.m.–12:03 p.m.

When Margaret heard the BMW pull out of the garage, she got up from the table and went to the window, the better to see her husband disappear down the street. Then she showered, carefully chose her underwear, skirt, blouse, jacket, and shoes, returned to the bathroom to put on her makeup and brush her hair, examined herself in the mirror, changed out of her skirt, jacket, and blouse into a little dress, changed the shoes, put on different jewelry, checked herself again in the mirror, took off the dress, put on a different skirt and this time a tight-fitting sweater and a third pair of shoes, went back to the original earrings and bracelets, added some pearls, removed the pearls, attached a pin to the sweater, looked again in the mirror, took off the sweater and put on a second blouse, repinned the pin, adjusted her hair, and went back down to the kitchen. Then she picked up the phone and called her office, told them she would not be coming in today but would be working off-site, picked up her purse, went into the garage, jumped into her MINI Cooper, tuned the radio to classical, and went on her way.

She would be driving out to Marin, meeting Peter at the Mountain Home Inn up on Mount Tam for a bit of brunch on the deck. Then they would leave one car behind on the mountain and drive together down the winding curves to Stinson Beach. It was a bit of a schlep to get to the Golden Gate Bridge from Twin Peaks, where she and Henry lived, and so it gave her time to think, not that she wanted to think. She wanted to get there, to see Peter, to start their day, their full day, their stolen day, their day in the sun, their day of being a real couple.

Or to feel like a real couple anyway. Such freedom! There was a little motel on the beach, nothing fancy—she swung onto Clarendon Avenue and then onto Seventeenth and then hung a right on Stanyan and followed it through the upper Haight, past the east edge of Golden Gate Park. She whizzed by house after house until the landscape suddenly gave way to shops and restaurants—she noted the American Cyclery shop, where years before she had purchased

Henry a beautiful white Bianchi that he rode maybe twice and then gave up because of the hills. She had dreamt they would put their bikes on the roof of the car and drive them out to Napa or Sonoma and ride from winery to winery or spend long Sunday afternoons in Golden Gate Park cycling all the way to Lands End—but it never happened. But that was then, and this was now, and she was already turning onto Park Presidio, which fed directly onto the bridge.

There was nothing really *wrong* with Henry. Aside from the neurosis of course, and that imagination that drove her crazy, and the fact that he accomplished virtually nothing he set his mind to. She had thought— But never mind. That was also long ago and not worth thinking about anymore.

She reached over to the back seat to make sure the package was there—the one she had hidden in case Henry looked into her car. Through the Tiffany bag she could feel the little box with its distinctive bow, and the card was there, too. A small wave of pleasure pulsed through her. She couldn't wait to present it to Peter. She would find just the right moment to make it perfect.

As she approached the bridge she was relieved there wasn't much traffic—she and Peter had timed it that way. It was now going on 10:00 a.m. and she'd be there in half an hour or so. To her right, the wide, smooth bay stretched out

toward Alcatraz and she could see all the way to the Berkeley Hills, though instantly she regretted looking because that
is where she met Henry. Sixteen years ago it was, waiting
outside a Chinese restaurant on Shattuck Avenue; she was
with her friend Dede, but she couldn't remember whom
he was with, just some guy, and they got to talking because
the wait was interminable, and before long he'd asked her
out, or maybe she asked him out offhandedly—"Hey, we're
going to a party later, want to come?"—but already in her
mind it was a date. She could even now vaguely recall how
exciting that was, the promise of hot, new love. He was tall,
cute, a little nerdy but trying his best to be brash. Sweet.
She was twenty-six then, forty-two now. She couldn't even
remember what she looked like then, couldn't even *imagine*
it anymore—the skin, the breasts, the ass of the twenty-
six-year-old Margaret. She'd never liked her body and still
didn't, but when she looked at old photos, she thought, My
God, that flat tummy! Her bosom had been high if not full,
and her legs weren't bad, either—but it was like a dream
because now all she could see was how thick her thighs had
become with the telltale mottling of cellulite and the disfigur-
ing webbing of veins that had begun to push up through the
plump skin. The rounding of her belly, the distinct drooping
of her breasts, which she had thought she would avoid since

she had never given birth, the sharpening of her neck into bony rivulets rising from her breastbone—all this was the burden she carried with her every moment of every day. Her body wasn't her temple—it was her tomb. But Peter told her she was beautiful, and she trembled at the thought of him.

Suddenly the traffic came screeching to a halt and she had to slam on the brakes. She waited a minute or two for the cars to start up again, but they didn't. No traffic coming from the other direction, either. Soon sirens could be heard rumbling up from San Francisco—ambulance, police cars, rescue. Drivers turned off their engines and stepped out onto the bridge. Even the pedestrians and bicyclists had been cordoned off and were not allowed to move forward. Margaret turned her car off, too, leaned out her window and called to some fellow standing beside his pickup, "Can you see what's happening?"

"Jumper!" he said.

"Are you serious?"

"I think so. That's what the guy in front of me said. I can't see anything myself."

Someone else had gotten up on the roof of his SUV, and Margaret yelled over to him, "Can you see?"

"Yeah," he yelled back, "they're all around the railing. I don't think the guy's jumped yet. I think maybe he changed his mind but is stuck or something. He's, like, hanging there."

"Jesus!" she said.

"It's a woman, actually."

"Jesus!" she repeated.

She looked at her watch and sighed. They had decided to meet at eleven, so she still had plenty of time, but for God's sake, why today, why now? But there was nothing to do about it, so she took out her phone, checked her e-mails, answered one or two of them, again checked to see what was going on outside, went back to her phone and played a game called Pet Rescue, checked the time again—ten thirty—turned the radio back on even without the motor running—Debussy—wrote another couple of e-mails— thought about Peter—and then decided she better call his cell. There was no answer, so she left a message: "You're not going to believe this, but there's a jumper on the bridge. I might be late. Please go ahead and order. Oh, I miss you!" Then she got out of the car and walked over to the guy who was still standing on his roof of his SUV.

"Anything happening yet?" she asked.

"I don't know."

"It seems to me if you want to kill yourself, go ahead," she said.

"Yeah, but what if it's some teenager? Or your brother or husband or sister?"

"Don't you think people should be able to do what they want?"

"You really believe we should let troubled people kill themselves?"

"I'm sure you're right," she said to mollify him, but what she was really thinking was, Hitler was troubled. Should we have stopped him from committing suicide? In any event, for her the question had been settled, and as she walked away she began to imagine what Peter would do when she finally arrived at the Mountain Home Inn, how his eyes would light up at the vision of her walking through the door, and how he would rise and embrace her and say, "I was so worried about you, darling," and how they would then sit across the table from each other, there on the sun-warmed deck that looked out over the mountains and all the way to the ocean. They would have eyes only for each other, his hand resting on her forearm, hers, under the table, on his thigh. But it was getting late and nothing was moving and even though the weather was beautiful, her nerves at this moment made it hard for her to enjoy what was actually in front of her—the panoramic city sparkling in the bright sun, the white sails on the gray waves, the flocks of gulls soaring over the waters, the endless blue of sky kissing the edge of the sea.

———

People just like to kill themselves at Christmas, she thought. It's a tradition, like drinking Tom and Jerrys. And we should let them. Christian charity and all.

As far as she was concerned there was something very stupid about Christmas, and not just the jumping off of bridges, and not even because Christmas was so commercial. She actually liked the commercial part, the window-shopping, the trees and houses strung with lights (although she was getting bored with the all-white-light thing and wouldn't mind a little color). She had no problem with the comforting old movies on TV, the magazine ads with automobiles wrapped in big red bows, the phony carolers at the mall, the bell-ringing Salvation Army Santas whom she assumed were mostly crackheads trying to stay clean, at least until the weekend. One could even experience a passing revival of religious feeling, fall in love with the Baby Jesus all over again and she was fine with that. No, it was that everyone put so much into it. That's what bothered her. As if all this crap really mattered. Everyone spent so much time thinking and worrying about Christmas and what to buy and where to go and whom to be with and if you were invited or not invited. And God forbid if you weren't jolly. It was a nightmare!

Perhaps she hadn't always felt this way, and, in truth, her cynicism made her cringe a little. Partly because it wasn't attractive, but also because she knew it wasn't entirely healthy. And indeed, there was a time when the holidays thrilled her. She even had a set of Christmas dishes in a box somewhere. Spode. With holly encircled by adorable little old-fashioned toys. She wanted to be that person again, the one who loved Christmas, the one who bought goofy china and silly ornaments and Santa place mats. They still had a tree, of course. Well, a little one. A silver one. Impossible to say what it was made of. Sat on the lowboy in the entry hall. Came with the ornaments already on it. Naturally Henry complained about it when she first brought it home, but he complained about everything. He couldn't abide change. But she knew he'd get over it because he got over everything.

They used to go up to Tahoe the week of Christmas. Not to ski, just to feel Christmasy, with the snow clinging to their boots and watching their breath plume in the icy air. They had to make reservations almost a year in advance. She reminded him to do it a million times until she realized she'd have to do it herself. Why fight? One year it was a cabin at Alpine, another it was a chalet in Kings Beach on the far north side of the lake. It was always so beautiful there. One could imagine oneself in a storybook or a movie. They even tried roasting chestnuts on an open fire. Never worked. Too mushy.

If the person is going to jump they should just get on with it! she thought. She did wish she had more patience, but it was hard on a day like today. Time, time was the precious thing.

Out over the bay, the sailboats seemed like stones set in a Zen garden, even though she knew they were actually moving, cutting and bouncing their way through the chop. It struck her that this disparity was really quite beautiful, the way distance makes things stand still, steals the life from them, the individuality, makes them part of some great tableau as the gods perhaps might see it. People might be making love down there on those boats, or fishing, or eating lunch, and it would seem so important to them and so real. But from this distance all the distractions of life evaporated like the fog that rolls in every morning—the obscuring fog of passion—and then is gone and what was left was a kind of preternatural clarity, a stoppage of time, an end to time, a vision of perfection. Although she wouldn't have minded one bit if the traffic started moving.

Just then her phone started ringing—she had left it on the seat of the car. She rushed to pick it up. Peter! At last!

But it was only her brother, Arthur.

———

"Oh God, Margaret!" were the first words out of his mouth.

"Hello, Arthur," she said.

"Oh, Margaret!"

"Calm down, sweetheart," she said, "and tell me what happened. I'm sure it's nothing so terrible."

"She broke up with me."

"Who? Who broke up with you?"

"Rita."

"Rita? What happened to what's her name—Lucy?"

"Lucy's still here."

"You were seeing Rita and still living with Lucy?"

"It's complicated," he said.

"Jesus, Arthur."

"Actually, Lucy broke it off."

"So it's *Lucy* who left."

"No, no, *Rita*. Rita broke it off, too. She's highly moral. She doesn't want to be responsible for wrecking my relationship with Lucy. You would not believe how ethical she is."

"I see."

"When we made love it was like two souls joining. It was like the whole world stopped and we were at the center of the universe—"

"I'm sure that's true, Arthur, but honestly, too much information."

"Maggie, we made love outside, under the stars, for hours and hours—"

"Arthur!"

"—in the woods, on the pine needles, looking at the Milky Way—"

"I really, really don't need to hear this."

"Well, we talked, too, if that's any help. For hours and hours. Oh, it was so much more than sex!"

"So, what you're saying is, you had sex with Rita in the woods—"

"In the backyard, actually."

"—and you told this to Lucy?"

"I wanted to be honest!" he said. "You know, ethical. Rita is incredibly ethical."

Margaret groaned, as she so often did when talking to her brother. "Well, maybe it's for the best," she said.

"It doesn't feel that way."

"Not now, but it will, my love."

"Oh, Margaret! I'm so unhappy."

"I know, dear."

"Can I come stay with you?"

"Oh, Arthur . . . I don't know . . ."

"Just for a few days."

"It's not the best time."

"She kicked me out, Margaret. Out onto the street."

"But it's *your* apartment, Arthur."

"It's complicated," he said.

"Just go to Lucy and tell her you want your apartment back."

"It's not Lucy. It's Rita."

"Rita has the apartment?"

"She won't let me back in."

"Arthur, it's *your* apartment."

"I could never kick her out. I wronged her. I have to protect her. You don't understand. Not that you should. How could you? How could anyone?"

"I think I can manage it. Just tell me."

"Come on," he begged. "Can't I just stay with you? It's Christmas, Margaret. It's Christmas."

"All right, all right. Calm down," she said. "I'll take care of it."

"I can come?"

"You're my brother, aren't you?"

"Bones will be okay with it, won't he?"

"Of course he will, Arthur. He loves you."

"He doesn't love me. He hates me."

"That's not true. He loves you. We all do.

"I love you, too, sis," he said.

So now she had to figure out a plan. First, she called United—she was Premier Platinum, so she used the direct line—and in ten minutes had him on a flight. Then she called him back and told him when to be at the airport—as it turned out he was already there, since he had no place else to go—and then Margaret had to face the unpleasantness of telling Henry. Unpleasant because she knew how he felt about Arthur, unpleasant because Bones hated surprises, unpleasant because she didn't want to ruin her day any more than it had already been ruined, and also unpleasant because she'd have to lie to him yet again. She didn't like lying. It was wrong. Although it did give her a little thrill. As usual, when she called his cell there was no answer and no voice mail, either, because he'd turned it all off. Only Henry turns off his voice mail. So after several tries she was forced to call the office line and face the scorn of Gladys, that idiot receptionist, and of course Gladys couldn't get through to him either, and with a tone

of supercilious commiseration offered to transfer Margaret to voice mail. The voice mail that was off. "No! I've
tried him three times. Go find him!" she commanded. And
when he finally did pick up, he was such a pill. Why he had
to put up such a fuss about everything was beyond her.
As if going to the airport was such a big deal. And as for
Arthur's alcoholism, that was total bullshit. He wasn't an
alcoholic. And he wasn't "psychotic," as Bones was always
insisting. He'd just made a few bad decisions and had a bit
of bad luck. It was the women he chose. Like that Lucy.
What a slut.

She noticed to her horror it was eleven fifteen, which
meant that even if the traffic started flowing that instant, she
wouldn't get to the Mountain Home Inn till almost noon.
She'd been on the bridge for more than an hour. She tried
Peter again, but still no answer. She tapped her fingers on
the steering wheel until they were numb from tapping.
She checked her e-mails again and then again. Nothing.
She looked at the time. She texted Peter. No response. She
looked at the time. Eleven thirty.

Half their day gone because some stupid asshole decided
it was okay to tie up the entire bridge with her angst. Well,
guess what? Everyone has angst. I have angst! The guy
standing on his Toyota has angst!

She bolted from the car, vaulted over the traffic barrier, bulldozed her way through the bleating crowd on the walkway, grasped the railing with both hands, leaned out as far as she could over the icy waters, craned her neck in the direction of the inept gaggle of police and firemen and medics, and screamed at the top of her lungs, "Let the fucking bitch jump!"

Her words echoed off the sea and bounced off the towers and cables, and from the crowd there rose such a roar of approval, such a loud round of applause, that the Golden Gate Bridge itself shook with laughter.

———

But it was still another half an hour before they'd talked the bitch down and the traffic started moving again, and then only one lane at a time.

CHAPTER 7

12:04–12:52 p.m.

When she finally emerged from the bridge, the traffic opened up as if there were never a problem, and she felt a charge of renewed pleasure as she climbed the Waldo Grade past the headlands. Once out of the tunnel, with its rainbow colors painted over its arched entrance like an upside-down smile, she began the descent into Sausalito. Marin County was a breath of fresh air, with its green vistas and forested hills. Its very strangeness brought her out of herself, reminded her she could be someone new. But why would she want to be someone new? What was wrong with the old Margaret? she wondered. Well, not wondered, exactly, because to wonder about oneself implied some sort of judgment. No, she simply wanted to examine.

Examine and observe. And what she observed was that, at least of late, she had been incredibly nice to her brother and horribly bitchy to her husband.

Henry suddenly appeared in her mind and said to her (in the way only Henry could): *Gosh, do you really think that's fair?* Meaning, why be nice to Arthur and not to him? This was something worth pondering because Margaret did sense there was something weird about it.

The truth was, if anyone in the triumvirate of Henry, Arthur, and her were a bit—let's say, *off*—it had to be Arthur. Yes, he was brilliant, no question about it—but he was also a college dropout who made his living mostly as a bartender. She firmly believed he'd dropped out because he was too smart for any ordinary undergraduate school. Why he didn't get into an Ivy she'd never understood, but that stupid George Dimwit University? She asked him a million times why he even applied there. Henry always rebuked her, saying you can get a good education anywhere. All you need is a library, and the teachers are just as good, too, and it's not Dimwit, it's Dinwoodie. But, honestly, all that was so besides the point. Arthur was advanced. Period. And because of one stupid miscalculation he never got to explore his deeper side. Their mother was partially to blame for that. She should have been much firmer with him. Should have taken him by the hand and made him do his damned applications.

Between Arthur and Henry it was like having two babies, and she could barely take care of one. At least Arthur was in Florida.

But God, he'd been a good-looking kid. The ladies even now swarmed all over him. He knew a million jokes. He could crack you up even if you'd heard them before. He'd recite entire scenes word for word from his favorite "golden age" movies (*The Godfather, Taxi Driver, Young Frankenstein*), and although sometimes it seemed to her he was hopelessly stuck in the '70s, it really was very entertaining. But the thing about Arthur that was most attractive—and most frustrating—was that he was a hopeless romantic. The quintessential optimist. Which one might think was a good thing. But it also meant he fell for a new bimbo every other week. She was always the *one*. The perfect love. Happy, happy, happy, forever and ever and ever!

And yet, Arthur could always make Margaret feel wonderfully good, incredibly special, as if she were the only person in the world. He did it with everyone, she knew that. But so had their father. It was a special gift. And no matter how bad things got, there was always some new horizon, some new opportunity just around the corner. "One door closes, another opens," Arthur always chirped when it seemed things could get no worse. Hadn't he encouraged her to become a real estate professional in those days when she felt horrible about herself? Hadn't he encouraged her to take those courses in Spanish? And sushi making? And pottery? Lately she'd been thinking of horseback riding, English, of course. He e-mailed her all kinds of links about it. Henry couldn't care less. And when she confessed rather sheepishly that she'd been shopping at Wilkes Bashford and Valentino, didn't he remind her how much she deserved it? Even if it was a lot of money, it was, after all, *Valentino*. "It's not like there won't be any more paychecks coming in!" he chided her. She never told Henry, but not because he'd put up a fuss. She was pretty sure he wouldn't. It was something else that stopped her, and she truly didn't know what. Henry went on and on about being a writer back when they first started, but nothing came of it. Arthur, on the other hand, wrote really good poetry, mostly about his girlfriends, and mostly lamentations, but he did write one for her once, on the occasion of her thirty-fifth birthday. He entitled it "Sister," and she cried when he read it to her. It was rhymed and everything.

Henry, on the other hand, used to bring up the guitar and croon out some carols on those Christmas weekends in Tahoe. Back then she hadn't the heart to tell him how bad his voice was. It was even possible she liked his singing— thinking it kind of sweet and romantic. Rose-colored glasses, she supposed. He used to make up stories, too. Or tried to. Delusions of creativity. Although when she thought about it, a measure of tenderness and even longing came over her. He would try to retell *A Christmas Carol* by replacing the characters with people they knew. His boss, for instance, was Jacob Marley and her brother was Tiny Tim and that woman they both hated who lived downstairs when they were on Mason Street, the old Italian lady—she became the Ghost of Christmas Past. The more he went on, the more absurd and convoluted and stupid it became. Then he'd switch to fairy tales. The one that always came to mind and even now brought a shudder to Margaret, was the one about the little orphan girl who was really a princess (named Margarita, of course) and all the wonderful and magical things that happened to her and how the frog or the stable boy would be freed from his curse by her kiss and how then he would be the knight (it was always Sir Henry) who restored her to her throne, only something about it made her feel queasy every time he got to this part.

"Why do *you* have to save *me*?" she would ask.

"But first you save me with your kiss. You see, it's, like, equal. I can't save you unless you save me."

"You don't have to save me," she said. "Nobody has to save me."

"It's just a story. But even if it weren't, why can't I help you? Don't you think love can transform a girl into a princess?"

"Oh, for Christ's sake!" she screamed, and fled into one of the empty bedrooms.

"Jeez," she heard him complain through the closed door. "What did I say?"

He never did get it. And when she'd brought home that ersatz Christmas tree a couple of years ago and he said, "What the hell is that?" she blurted, "Stop being such a pussy."

"But it's Christmas . . ."

She slammed the miserable little whatever-it-was-made-of bush on the table. "It's a fucking tree. Deal with it."

Naturally, he went off to sulk. It took but fifteen minutes for him to emerge with that vapid smile of his and concede, "Well, actually it's not so bad."

The thing is, even though she'd known when she was buying the damned thing in the five-and-dime exactly how events at home would transpire, Henry's response turned into a revelatory moment for her. Because it was not her intention, and it was certainly not her desire, to be cruel. What she did desire, quite simply, was for Bones, her husband, the man with whom she had elected to spend her entire life, to—*just once*—stand his ground.

Henry seemed so perfect when she'd first met him. It was as if she'd wandered into a rose garden of a thousand varieties she'd never seen before and Henry was the most beautiful of them all. There was a fragrance in this garden, something ineluctable, something just beyond her field of experience but she nevertheless could feel with senses she'd never explored, as if her skin could hear, her eyes could feel, her ears could see, as if all the senses of her body were one, and the whole of her was vibrating with sensation. Whatever it was, it was overwhelming, and she was swallowed up in a happiness so unfamiliar it made her dizzy. All those petals opening before her, all those colors, all those scents inviting her to fall into his garden. The garden of Lethe, she ultimately realized, for indeed a kind of forgetfulness had come over her—she forgot her fears, her ambition, forgot the faults of her body and the very laws of reality by which she had tried to live her whole young life. In this strange state she felt she could fly, could melt, could flow outside the river of necessity. It was frightening, and yet she did not want it to stop.

It must have been that stupid, openhearted laugh of his that got her, that wide, innocent smile that she now saw as merely insipid. How could she have fallen for that? But really, what defense did she, a mere girl, have against those soul-searching eyes? Back then, they were the eyes of Adonis, the most beautiful of the gods, and his laugh was the laugh of Dionysus, god of wine and passion, about whom she vaguely remembered reading in a class she'd once taken on mythology. If she had had the slightest of brains, she would have put the brakes on right then and there. But why berate herself now? She was just a dumb kid, a little honeybee buzzing around the nectar of love.

And he was so tall and strange and awkward. The distressed jeans, the Doc Martens lace-up boots. He even had an AC/DC T-shirt! She couldn't imagine Peter ever wearing anything like it, thank God. But the memory was kind of sweet, anyway.

She never could quite shake that first conversation they had, God, so long ago. Sixteen years this past summer. It stuck to her like chewing gum on the bottom of her shoe.

They'd gone back to that Chinese restaurant after the party because they never did have dinner. It must have been an all-night joint because it was late. In her mind's eye, she could see him sitting across from her, his hands wrapped around one of those Chinese teacups with no handle.

"So, Henry," she ventured, trying as always in those days to deflect the conversation away from herself.

"Bones," he corrected her.

"You majored in English lit? What good did that do you?"

"Even worse. Creative writing."

"Oh."

"Yeah."

"No, that's cool," she said. "Creative writing."

"Double major with philosophy. But I love to write," he explained. "I love the way the words go down on paper. There's something magical about it. Or musical. Or both. I don't know. Mystical. All the 'M' words." He laughed.

"I can't write to save my life," she said.

"Sure you can."

"No, I can't. It's like pulling teeth. I start with these great ideas, like, for a term paper or a journal entry or whatever, but then, like, I don't know. Thank God I'm done with term papers."

"Hmm," he mused.

"Hmm, what?"

"No, no, I'm not being judgmental. I just want to know more," he said. "I'm interested."

"There is nothing more."

"Sure there is."

"I just said there wasn't."

"I know you said that. I'm actually listening to what you're saying. But there is more."

"I don't know where you're going with this," she said, shrinking at the sharpness of her tone. She looked up to see what damage she'd done, but he was just sipping his tea.

"Do you mind if I ask you a question or two?" he said.

She hesitated.

"That's okay," he said. "Never mind."

"No, no, go ahead."

"So when you sit down to write, what happens?"

"I don't know. I just go blank."

"But, Margaret, that's what you should do. In fact, that's perfect. Blankness is the perfect state of mind."

"No, it's not."

"It is. Just don't let it scare you."

"It doesn't scare me."

"That's what's stopping you."

"What is?" she asked.

"You don't admit you're afraid."

"That's not true," she said, averting her eyes. She could feel her stomach start to cramp. And then, weirdly, her right leg began to tremble.

She waited for him to say something. Tell her what's what. Fix it. But when she looked up he was still just sitting there waiting, enjoying his tea.

She had the terrible urge to say something funny, or at least try to explain herself—but something stopped her and that something was, simply, Henry. Because he just sat there waiting. Hands on the cup of tea. Chopsticks resting on the folded napkin. Teapot white and bulbous. Water glasses beading from the ice. Little jars of soy sauce and vinegar. It was all like a Vermeer, uncannily still, shimmering with color, every detail held to the light just for her.

"I really don't know what I mean," she finally said. "I don't know what's true and what's not true."

"See, I think that's great," he replied, with a voice as gentle as the rain that had begun falling beyond the big plate glass windows of the restaurant. "You've just opened yourself up to whatever is actually happening inside you. If you took a pencil now and started to write, you'd write."

"Yeah," she said, "and I'd hate it."

"So what? So what if you hate it?"

"What do you mean?"

"It doesn't matter if you like it or not. It just matters that it's coming from you, from inside *you*. At least that's what matters to me."

And then, in spite of the fact that they had not yet ordered anything to eat, she said, "You want to get out of here?"

———

Where had this gone? Where had *he* gone? How could it all have changed so much? She fiddled with the radio. She used to have an old Volvo. The radio was so simple. The MINI required an advanced degree just to find a decent station. She was on Sirius and wanted to switch to AM to check the traffic but somehow ended up with blues. Henry could not resist the blues. Put on the blues and Henry got all African American on you, lowering his voice and everything. But actually it was Arthur who had become quite blue lately. It was long in coming. So many things hadn't worked out for him, and how long can a person stay hopeful? She could feel his sadness—and it wasn't about the girls he went through. It was something else, something corrosive, like he had fallen into a vat of self-doubt. He was putting himself down a lot these days. That never happened before. And on top of everything, Arthur had gotten fat. Extremely fat. Like almost three-hundred-pounds fat.

No wonder it had become harder and harder for Arthur to feel the exuberance for which he was so admired. He admitted once that it was too hard to climb the stairs to his bedroom, so he fell asleep most nights on the recliner in the TV room.

Henry reminded her that there were no stairs in his apartment and no TV room, either. It was a junior one-bedroom. "It's because he drinks the better part of a bottle every night," Henry insisted.

"Can you blame him?" she said. "Can you blame him?"

The trouble really started when Arthur got his hands on the inheritance. It wasn't all that much, just a little nest egg, so paltry Mother actually apologized for it on her deathbed. "Your father didn't leave all that much, really, in spite of what you think, and then, well, I needed it," she wheezed.

But small as it was, it was more than enough to get Arthur into trouble.

Margaret had urged him to invest it.

"I *am* investing," he declared.

She was thrilled. "So who's going to manage it for you? Fidelity? Schwab?"

"The best in the business!"

For some years, Arthur, explained, he'd been enthralled by an infomercial that had been appearing on one of the shopping channels. "It's like, foolproof. We should go in on it together."

"You're kidding," she said. "An infomercial?"

"It's called Investomatic! Check out their website. Investomatic! With an exclamation mark at the end."

She immediately brought it up on her screen and read: Created by the world's most successful investors! Automatically trade stocks like a professional! Just five minutes of your time a day! Earn 10, 15, even 20 percent a month! Take our FREE introductory course and make your financial dreams come true—today!

"It's really easy," he said. "I took the course."

And indeed, after taking the free introductory course, the Investomatic! system required almost nothing of him. Aside from coughing up fifteen hundred for the DVDs, booklets, online briefings, 24-7 chat line, daily "for your eyes only" e-mail tips, and the "proprietary" Investomatic! trading software, all he had to do was go to their site every morning and look at a bunch of green and red arrows. A massive amount of greens? Buy! Too many reds? Sell!

"Arthur, that's day-trading. It's the worst thing you can do. Nobody makes money day-trading. You have to constantly be on top of it. You have to really know what you're doing."

"No, these guys have got everything. You should see their charts! Really, really cool. The moving averages. The stochastics. The indicators. The volume."

"Do you even know what those things are?"

"Of course I do. They teach you all that stuff."

"You really went to classes?"

"More like a video."

For the next few weeks Arthur was the main topic at Henry and Margaret's house, breakfast, dinner, and bedtime.

Finally he said, "Margaret, just do something about it."

"He's a grown man, Bones, what can I do? Anyway, I don't know why I'm so worried. He's so smart."

"I know. He's a fucking genius."

"Why do you always have such a negative take on him?"

"Me? You're the one going on and on."

"It's his inheritance. The money my father slaved for."

"Here we go with your father again."

"You just hate Arthur."

"Honestly, I don't. But I do hate the drinking."

"He's under pressure."

"He's out of control."

"Well then, talk to him."

"Me? What could I tell him that you haven't told him?"

"You're a man. He'll listen to you."

"Right."

"He will."

Henry sighed. He was always sighing.

"If he ends up coming here to live," Margaret told him, "you'll have no one to blame but yourself."

In the end, though, Margaret didn't trust Henry to say the right thing. So once again she was forced to fix things. Thank God she still had power of attorney over the inheritance, even Arthur's half. Mother had seen to that. When reason didn't work with Arthur—when did it ever?—she just went ahead and stopped the bleeding. Arthur was livid, and this pained her, but she felt she was doing exactly what her father would have done, and he was rarely wrong.

In retrospect, she saw that this was when Arthur went into his hole. She had to ask herself if she had done wrong by him. She looked at it from every angle, and in the end

decided she was right to hold firm. Otherwise she would have been letting him down as Mother had.

———

Now as she was driving down 101, rounding the curve at the Rodeo Avenue exit, she wanted to know why she never got mad at Arthur, never yelled, never told him he was a fool—because that thought never crossed her mind. As the MINI descended toward Mill Valley, and the wild hills and the bay gave way to shopping centers and low-rise apartments, she asked herself, Why did she forgive him everything? And why could she not forgive Henry anything?

Her shrink told her it most likely had to do with her father.

"I don't think so," Margaret had said.

"You don't think your father—"

"Haven't we already talked about my father? It seems like we've talked and talked about him."

"Is that how it feels to you?"

"Yeah."

"Would you like to talk about him now?"

"I don't know where to start," she'd said.

"How about the first thing that comes into your mind?"

But the first thing that came into her mind was that she almost missed her exit, coming as it does so soon after you come down the hill. And why was she worrying about all this old stuff when she was on her way toward the new, the bright, and the wonderfully beautiful?

———

As she approached Tam Junction (right to Mill Valley, left to Mount Tamalpais—hurray!) the phone rang again. She knew by the ring it was the office—Matt Hoffman, the chief investment officer at Regency Development. He was also the main bean counter. What now? she thought. She'd called in sick but foolishly told them she would be working at home. You always say you'll be working at home. Nobody believes you. But Matt was a big muckety-muck at Regency and she was just a vice president in residential development. Even as recently as two months ago she wasn't sure it would work out. Yet here she was, a breath away from full partner. She had to laugh, remembering her first days in real estate. She was selling $500,000 homes way out in the Avenues to mostly Asians and Latinos. It didn't take long for her to realize she could make a hell of lot more money selling houses in the Marina District to young up-and-comers or in Pacific Heights to the already well-heeled. She finagled an inter-

view at Hill and Co., got a job, and soon was a top producer. She knew why, too. There was more to selling than being a salesman, more even than arranging the financing and navigating escrow. It was all about allaying fears; and the way to do that was to befriend your clients. To make it fun. To let them understand they weren't in it alone. But more than that, you had to *know* your client—and this was her specialty. When she was working in the Marina, she understood the echo-boomer. Nowadays she'd made herself an expert on millennials. She studied them, analyzed them, hung with them, catered to them—which is why she drove a MINI and not a Mercedes like every other fucking agent in the world.

Her life really changed when she got the call from Charlie Oates. He was an old-timer, an independent who liked to buy and sell and occasionally do a rehab. He was deep into a loft conversion on Townsend and didn't know how to appeal to young people. He'd heard about her, he'd said. "Yeah, well I haven't heard of you," she'd said. When he told her about the project she realized the whole concept was shit, and she told him so. The apartments were too big. No place for bicycles. No amenities like top-drawer kitchens. He begged her to come work for him. "Why the hell should I do that?" she said. "Because if we close this thing out, you will be very, very richly rewarded." The *promote*,

Charlie called it. The payoff. One year later, every unit in that building was sold and she was, indeed, considerably richer.

And this was in 2009, the worst part of the Great Recession. Now everyone knew who Margaret Quantum was. They did an article about her in the *Chronicle*.

It was after Charlie's second conversion—an old icehouse on Delancey Street that she topped out in six weeks (six weeks! thirty-six units! 1.1 million for a lousy 700-square-foot one-bedroom)—that she got the call from Regency.

Now she was dealing not in the millions but hundreds of millions. At Regency they created entire neighborhoods, built huge office complexes. There was a unit that dealt only with medical buildings. Another that focused on retail. She was currently in residential and mixed-use, but she made sure she was part of the Market Street renaissance that was now going on between Fifth and Ninth Streets. What with Twitter, Spotify, Yelp, and a bunch of other youth-oriented companies moving their offices there, she reasoned, those overpaid millennials would need a place to live, wouldn't they? She had in her mind a new kind of apartment building. It would be totally wired for every possible online application, down to regulating the air-conditioning, turning on your lights, locking your door and, if possible, tucking you in at night; it would be 100 percent green, 50 percent solar, totally water-conserving, recycling eco-masterpiece. In fact, it would be built of largely recycled materials (that number eventually went down to 10 percent, but whatever); it would be super friendly, with easy sharing of whatever you wanted to share, because that's what millennials were all about. Furnishings? Incredibly hip. Italian kitchens, Japanese soak tubs, in-apartment bike storage, undercounter wine coolers—even retro-looking appliances if you wanted. Not to mention the rooftop pool and outdoor party space with retractable roof, and, somewhere nearer the ground floor, the communal kitchen and wet bar and a couple of faux-rustic dining rooms with those long farmhouse tables for dinner parties too big for your apartment. She practically wanted to live there herself, and if she weren't married, and maybe five years younger, she would have.

Even so, she presented her ideas to the development committee in a very restrained and rational manner, her voice, as always, contained and precise, letting the numbers she had so assiduously researched and vetted speak for themselves. She delineated the construction cost, pretty much to the penny (not that anyone could hold her to that), and did an analysis of the market that was so detailed half the people fell asleep. She was unhappy about that because she'd spent so much time putting together the animated graphs, the interviews with potential buyers, the lifestyle montage, all set to a contemporary playlist. But when she got to her projections for return on investment, everyone was awake again and smiling.

It was a thing of beauty.

And when she got the go-ahead, she knew if she pulled it off she'd get partner. Executive VP, for sure, or even higher. Director of Residential Development, for instance. This is what happens, she told herself, when you're a man of action.

And if you're a man of action, you answer your phone, especially if it's your superior calling. The annoyance was that she'd failed to put on her Bluetooth, which meant she'd have to pull over, which meant being even later for Peter, but what could she do? Luckily there was a little shopping center just before the junction. She pulled in and found a spot.

"Hey, hi!' she began in her most enthusiastic voice.

"Sorry you're not feeling well," Matt said.

"Yeah," she replied, deciding not to cough.

"There are just a few things I need to go over today. I'm really sorry."

He wasn't sorry in the least. And honestly, she understood. Just like Matt, she was at the office ten, twelve hours a day, and you have to get done what you have to get done. She definitely would call someone who's sick. Or on vacation, why not? The worst thing she could imagine was not performing. You just don't do that. If your work doesn't shine every single moment, what value are you?

"I'm not *that* sick," she said to Matt. "What's up?"

There was a problem. It had to do with a series of cost projections that had changed in the months since her presentation, and it was really annoying because the guys she'd entrusted this to were fucking around with various scenarios that only confused things, plus they kept adding contingencies.

"Here's the thing," he said. "You want to make the units smaller so you can have more of them, right?"

"Millennials *want* small units. It's not me. It's them."

"But that means more walls. Walls cost money. And if there's more density because there are more units, you have the whole higher level of fire-code enhancements. Which means the cost per square foot goes up by—well, your guys have given me four different sets of numbers. What am I supposed to do with that?"

"Wow, Matt," she said, "thank you for bringing this to my attention." By which she meant, Jesus fucking Christ, why does this always happen with you money guys? I'm going to get my extra units no matter what you say, so chill the fuck out. "You know," she went on brightly, "I thought something like this might happen. No biggie. You'll have revised figures by tomorrow."

"Great," he said.

"But I have to ask, Matt—are you completely happy with that engineering team they assigned me? I know they've done stuff for us in the past—"

"Why?"

"I mean, have you ever worked with them before? These multiple projections are not professional. I mean, they're good guys, but jeez. What do you suggest? You know what? I'll have a talk with them. Get them back on the right track."

"Okay. Whatever you think."

Matt had a laundry list of other items he wanted to cover, too, and droned on for an eternity. She actually did listen, because one had to be on top of everything, but she didn't bother to take notes. Didn't have to. She knew what he was going to say before he said it. Which meant she could continually stare at her watch, tap her feet on the floorboard, and roll her eyes.

When he was finally done, she said, "Got it. Not to worry," and he said, "Thanks, Madge. Now go back to sleep. And don't forget the chicken soup and ginger ale!"

People called her Madge at work. She never corrected them.

"No problem," she said. "I'm sure I'll be better by tomorrow. And, Matt," she added, "I'm really glad we had this conversation."

———

She edged the car back onto Shoreline Drive and made the left toward Tamalpais and the Mountain Home Inn, where, she hoped, Peter was still being held captive. Another twenty fucking minutes down the tube. It was a beautiful drive, though, and had she been less frantic about Peter, perhaps she might have enjoyed it, as she used to when she and Bones came here on weekends. They would take the route past the Zen Center at Green Gulch and promise themselves they were definitely going to go there on a retreat and then break out laughing because they never actually did, though years later Henry did go, only alone. Sometimes she and Henry would end up at the Pelican Inn in Muir Beach, where they would have bangers and meat pies because it was supposed to be an English pub. It was indeed dark and wainscoted and Tudoresque, and in those days it seemed charming to her. Sometimes they would take a room.

Today, she'd be taking a different route, thank God, turning off at Panoramic and heading up the mountain.

Just as she was about to make the turn onto Panoramic she noticed a rather ragged young couple with their thumbs out standing at the crossroads in front of the signs for Stinson and Mount Tam. He had a reddish beard and blond hair and was wearing shorts. She had long brown hair and wore light blue jeans and a tank top. Idiots, she thought. They think California is sunshine.

They looked so fragile that, in spite of her rush, Margaret stopped, rolled down her passenger window, and cried out over the engine noise, "Where are you going?"

"We're trying to get to Muir Woods. Which way is it?"

"Either way will get you there," she replied. "I could take you partway, but you'd have to get another ride at the turnoff."

"That's fine, that's fine," they said with brightest of smiles, as if she were the wizard Gandalf and they were Frodo and Sam trying to find safe passage into the land of Mordor.

"It's a very small car. And you're very tall," Margaret said to the boy.

"We'll squeeze!" said the girl with the long hair. She laughed and threw her arm around the boy.

"Honestly, you'd be better waiting for someone going to Muir Woods," said Margaret.

"Oh." They took a couple of steps back, their smiles fading. "Well, thanks anyway."

"Okay, okay, never mind. Get in."

Elated, the girl jumped in the narrow rear seat, sliding behind Margaret so that her boyfriend could push his own seat all the way back to accommodate his long legs.

"MINI Cooper," he said, running his hands across the leather. And indeed, the car was so small he had to jam his pack between his lap and the dashboard. He sort of disappeared behind it, except for his head, which was large, hairy, and very animated. The girl, meanwhile, spread out on the back seat, thrusting one leg toward the passenger side and resting her head on the shoulder of the front seat.

"Where are you two from? Obviously not from here," Margaret asked a bit nervously. She had never, ever, ever, picked up hitchhikers.

"We're both at NYU. Winter break."

"Not going home for Christmas?"

"Not this year."

"Your parents must not be happy about that."

"Yeah," they said.

They drove along a bit. Margaret couldn't believe her own moxie. To pick up hitchhikers. To have no fear. She checked out the girl in the rearview and then looked over at the boy. He had a strong aroma about him—not exactly body odor, but something less than clean. It was thick and the car filled up with it.

"Have you two been going out long?" she asked, thinking of nothing else to say.

"We're more like friends," the girl said.

"Oh. You seem so natural together. Like a couple."

The girl laughed, and the boy looked over his shoulder at her and smiled. The odor intensified with his movements. It was weird. She kind of liked the smell.

"Ooo, what's this?" cried the girl, holding up the little blue box in her soiled fingers. "Who's going to get Tiffany's for Christmas?"

"Just someone," said Margaret.

"Lucky someone!"

"My secret lover," Margaret, much to her amazement, suddenly announced. "I'm going to see my secret lover. He's getting Tiffany."

"Wow. Really?"

"Yep."

Again the boy looked over his shoulder at the girl, then at Margaret.

"I'm having an affair," she continued baldly. "I'm going to see him now."

"Uh, you're married?"

"Yep."

"To someone else?"

"Yep."

"So, it's, like, an affair."

"Yep."

"Wow," he said again.

From the back seat, the girl squeezed forward, her chin on her elbows. "So, like, does your husband know?" she asked. They were interested now, perhaps excited even.

"Uh, *no*," said Margaret.

"So you're like, what? Going to his house?"

"The beach."

"You mean like right there on the beach?"

"No, no. We have a motel. More of an inn, I think."

The boy scratched his beard. "Too conventional," he said. "You don't want a motel. You want . . ."

"A teepee," said the girl.

He laughed. "Too small. How about a bomb shelter? Nobody has an affair in a bomb shelter."

"No view," said Margaret. And everyone laughed.

After a few moments the girl said, "You're kidding right? About the affair?"

"Of course."

"I thought so."

"Was it that obvious?"

"I don't know. You don't seem the type. You seem too nice."

"We're here," Margaret said, pulling over to the shoulder. "Just down that road. You can probably walk it in half an hour, but there will be a million cars."

"Great, thanks," said the boy.

"I would have taken you down, but I'm late."

"For your affair?"

"Never too late for an affair," she quipped. "Although in this case, I think I may be."

As the girl got out of the car she turned back, leaned through the window, and placed her hand on Margaret's arm. "It was fun driving with you," she said. "Be safe. I'm sure whoever's getting that gift will love it."

And with that, Margaret threw the car in gear and headed up toward the Mountain Home Inn, checking the back seat to make sure the little blue box was still there.

CHAPTER 8

Peter barely said a word when Margaret stepped out onto the deck where he'd been sitting for almost two hours with only a heat lamp as company. On the table before him were a dirty plate and a crumpled napkin. She wanted to kiss him, but he turned aside, and she had to content herself with his cheek.

"I'm glad you didn't wait," she said.

"Didn't wait? I've been waiting hours."

"No, I mean about brunch."

"I couldn't just sit here taking up a table."

"No, it's fine."

The waitress came up, all smiles, and handed Margaret a menu.

"Oh!" said Margaret. "Can't I still have breakfast?"

"I doubt it, but I'll check."

"Oh, don't check—let's just live large!"

"In the meantime, can I get you something to start?" asked the waitress. "Wine? Coffee?"

"Let's have mimosas," she said.

"One or two?" asked the waitress.

Margaret looked hopefully at Peter. He barely glanced up at her.

"Two," she said, and then to him, "Oh, come on, grumpy, it wasn't my fault. Didn't you get my messages?"

"Yeah. I finally got a signal."

"Look, I wasn't the one who was jumping. Though I did think about it!"

"Two hours," he said.

"I know, sweetheart. I'm sorry. Let's not waste a minute more."

She was just grateful he was at least still there, grumpy or not. She herself wouldn't have waited so long. And how exposed he had been, sitting out on this deck all by himself, having to worry about taking up a table, not having a book to read or anything to do, no computer or anything. And all around him tourists and newlyweds, because during the week that's all there were, the hikers and locals appearing only on weekends, which, of course, was the reason they had chosen the place, but just to be surrounded by couples and all alone. . . . He probably played Pet Rescue, too. In that way, at least, they were together. Although she recalled he actually preferred gambling games like Vegas Slots or some such.

Her heart went out to him. She loved the way he pouted, the tinge of fire in his eyes, the way he took her for granted. She dared to place one hand on his leg and let her fingers slide up toward his groin.

"Isn't that better?" she said.

"So, tell me what happened," he finally asked.

"The bitch wouldn't jump," she replied. "She was just plain chickenshit, wasted everyone's time." She burst out laughing. "Now she'll have to spend twenty years in a loony bin." She squeezed his crotch. "God, I'm starving!" She felt him grow a little hard, and this encouraged her, because how long can a guy stay mad with a girl squeezing his dick?

She didn't tell him about the twenty minutes talking to Matt. He would see it as weakness, not being able to stand up to your boss, not being your own man, or being so attached to your job you didn't really have a life.

She sipped her mimosa and ordered a frittata and begged Peter to also order something, so he dutifully requested a dessert—whichever one you like best, he said to the waitress—and out came a huge slice of chocolate layer cake, which he seemed to enjoy, and Margaret ate her frittata and the side of fruit. She drank a second mimosa, which was risky because she was not much of a drinker, but she felt she really needed that second one, and she implored Peter to have one as well—even though she knew she was forcing it on him and she didn't like how that made her look, but she did it anyway because she believed it would help him loosen up and get them back to where they were supposed to be. And she was right, of course, because she was almost always right. Peter's shoulders softened, and his eyes became a little dreamy, and when he finally reached out and touched the skin of her forearm, she knew all would be well. He caressed her arm with the same searching movements she used on his cock. I win, she thought.

"I picked up a couple of kids on their way to Muir Woods. They reminded me of us. So in love."

"And how long did that take?" he asked.

She touched him on the nose. "Nothing could keep me away from you, sweetheart."

Much of Peter's appeal came from his looks alone. He was stout and a little brutish, with a patrician face and moppish blond hair falling over his left eye—a prep-school brat through and through. Fucking him was kind of like fucking Jack Kennedy. He even wore a rep tie and in summer a seersucker suit, and she decided he was well-read even though he never talked books or, in fact, ever seemed to read anything other than the *Wall Street Journal*. He was also a little sloppy around the seams, but in a charming country-doctor sort of way; his shirts sometimes came untucked and his tie was often off-kilter. Only people with old money looked like that, she decided, though actually he was in insurance and had a degree from San Jose State. Henry had gone to the University of Chicago, and a lot of good that had done him. All he learned to do was think. Think and think and think. But why was she bringing up Henry anyway? For the entire past week, all she had thought about was Peter, and now she was thinking about Bones? Do I feel guilty? she asked herself right then and there. Well, perhaps she did a little. After all, Henry wasn't a horrible person. It was just that she couldn't stand him anymore. Not that she could say exactly why, just that everything he did was so annoying. Sometimes she watched him dress, or eat, or watch TV, or read a book, and she was disgusted. Really disgusted to the point of wanting to vomit. Had she felt this way about Henry before she met Peter?

Maybe it was the thing in Chicago. Maybe it went all the way back to that. All the way to the very beginning.

She knew Henry had been accepted in a PhD program at the University of Chicago before she'd met him and that their whole getting together was just a fluke. He was in San Francisco visiting a friend. Not much of a friend because she never saw him again. The two of them were hanging out or something before going on to graduate school. Margaret herself had been out of college for a couple of years. Actually, she'd never finished. She'd been switching majors so many times she never had enough hours. So she took a job as a waitress, a receptionist, a salesgirl in a small dress shop in North Berkeley, whatever came along. Henry intended to stay with his pal for a week, but after he met Margaret he ended up staying the whole month, mostly with her, sometimes back in San Francisco. He told her she was funny and smart and cute, but she realized there was also something about her that seemed to put him off. He never really opened up. Maybe it was that hypercritical thing she did. She thought of it as having "high standards," but it often came out as a put-down, supercilious and even nasty. More likely, it was her neediness that frightened him. For the life of her, she didn't know why she acted this way around him. Could she really have been such a needy person? She hated this part of herself more than she hated the critic. Something about *him*. It was obviously because of him. She could see for herself how she sort of glommed on to him, wouldn't let him out of her sight, always asking him where he'd been or where he was going or who he had been socializing with. It was pathetic.

In the beginning Henry reminded her a little of her father, who had also been tall and thin and dark-haired, though never disheveled or absent-minded. But Henry was smart and articulate and generous. She saw him as a guy who knew what he wanted in life, someone who could take care of things. She showered him with affection. She pouted when he went off on his own.

She hoped her attentions flattered him. He did sometimes puff up when she'd ask his opinion on the most trivial of things, but he seemed to have a natural desire to be kind. They laughed a lot and he said she was very, very sexy. She told him she'd do whatever he wanted. And maybe she would have, too, but he never asked for anything all that special. Mostly kissing and cuddling.

But that magical August came to an end and Henry had to pack his bags and go east to Chicago. She put him on BART but didn't go with him to the airport—he said he didn't want her to. The doors hissed shut, hermetically separating them for what they both figured was a final good-bye, and the train almost silently pulled away. He barely had time to wave. She walked home along Shattuck—she lived in a dilapidated Victorian with six other ex-students on Dwight—passing the Indian and Chinese and Thai and Vietnamese eateries that were the staple of so many college kids, the video stores, the bookstores, the little clothing stores, the bars. "Oh well," she said to herself, "that's that," and went inside for a beer.

Looking back, she was shocked at how immature she had been, how rudderless, barely recognizable as the Margaret she eventually became. She honestly hadn't even noticed how flaky and inconsequential her life was until Henry pointed it out in that kind of Asperger's way he sometimes had about him—stating the obvious about something no one with an ounce of social grace would do: "You're just treading water," he said, "flailing about, you're not doing much of anything, are you? Don't you want to *be* someone?" She cringed when he said these things, and she cringed now remembering them.

The day after he flew to Chicago she went out to find a real job, even though she hadn't a clue how. She first went to an employment agency but all they had were clerical and sales. She thought the student counseling service might help, but she had no degree and no skills, and she wasn't a student anymore anyway. Then she remembered this guy who owned a nursery or something over in Oakland, and he said, "Sure, come on, I'll train you," but on the third day of struggling to remember the names of hundreds of plants and flowers, getting soaked and muddied in the seed beds, and lugging stinking bags of compost, she dragged herself home, threw herself on the bed, and began to sob. It was one of the very few times in her life this happened, but it was a doozy. She couldn't stop for at least an hour. It was then she knew she missed Henry, missed him enormously, with every particle of her soul and every fiber of her body. It was crazy. She barely knew him.

She couldn't help wondering what he was doing at that very moment. He hadn't called or written. Possibly he even said he wouldn't, she couldn't remember. She checked the time. Six. It was already night in Chicago. No doubt he was out with friends. Or maybe he'd already found a girlfriend. The women at the University of Chicago were all brainy like he was. Nerdy like he was. They were focused and determined and squared away and, based on how she imagined they looked, man-hungry. She wanted to talk to him. Had to talk to him. But she didn't know the phone number of his residence hall. Nobody had cell phones back then. Christ, she thought now, if they had, none of this would have happened.

She remembered the sleepless nights like it was yesterday, and how one morning she worked up the courage to call the Philosophy Department because that's really all she knew to do, but the assholes wouldn't give her his number. They did let slip the name of his dorm, though, which she scribbled on the back of her hand. They assured her they'd pass the message to him, but she knew they wouldn't. They'd forget. Or he wouldn't come by the office. Why would he? He'd go to class. He wouldn't go to the department office.

That's why she got on an airplane and showed up at his door around dinnertime the next day.

"Hi!" she said, all smiles. "Surprise!"

"Margaret!"

"That's me!" she said.

"Huh!"

"I just kinda wanted to see where you lived," she chirped.

"Really?"

"No. I came all this way just to stand on a street corner." She instantly regretted her tone. Henry, thank heaven, hadn't seemed to notice it.

"Oh, sorry, sorry," he said. "Come on in. Come in! I just didn't—"

"That's what a surprise is. It surprises you."

"Well, you did a great job there," he said.

She lowered her eyes, shuffled her feet. "Did I make a mistake?" she asked contritely. "This was really stupid, wasn't it? I'm an idiot."

"No, no," he said.

"Who would want someone like me to show up at their doorstep?"

"It's fine. It's fine." But his eyes suddenly grew wide. "Uh, is that a suitcase?"

"Just an overnight bag."

"Oh, good."

"Oh dear!" she cried, moisture forming in the corners of her eyes.

"No, I mean, 'Oh *good*—you have a change of clothes at least!' "

She smiled and kissed him on the cheek.

He grabbed her suitcase, which of course was much too big to be an overnighter, and led her up to his room, describing the place as he went. There were students from all over the world, he said, postgrads mostly. Library here, media room down there, kitchen in the basement, I'm on the fourth. It seemed to her a horrible place, far worse than her house in Berkeley, which at least had the charm of a genteel dilapidation. This was a desolate, gray, Gothic monstrosity, sunless and claustrophobic. Whatever charm it might have had was eradicated by layers of modernization, barren stretches of Formica and vinyl. The narrow halls echoed as they walked, and there was a dark smell of too many bodies, of pizza and bratwurst, textbooks and laundry. At least he had his own room, but it was tiny, a miniature of a room. And what a mess. Clothes thrown everywhere, books piled on the floor, bed unmade, a sliver of a window you might find in a jail cell.

"Hey, nice!" she exclaimed. "I like it."

"It's kinda small," he said, "but what do I need with big? It's just me."

"It's not that small," she replied, and, in a move so fast and agile it amazed even her, she yanked her blouse over her head and exposed her bare breasts. Her nipples were hard as rocks, so hard and extended they hurt. It embarrassed her, but she stood there without so much as a quiver, crumpled blouse dangling from one hand, eyes dilated and fixed upon his, lips soft and, she hoped, glistening with the lip gloss she'd applied just before going into the building.

"My God," he finally said. "What a woman!"

———

She could feel the old sweetness come over him, the way he cuddled her afterward, the way he asked her if she were hungry, the way he ran to get her something to drink from the Coke machine. Whatever it was that she had feared now dropped away, as if she had thrown off a heavy winter coat. She washed his sheets and made his bed, organized his drawers and closet, created a nice shelf for his books, unpacked her bag and put her clothes away in spaces she had set aside for herself. Most lovely of all, he never once asked her how long she was going to stay.

A few weeks later the Resident Head on his floor informed Henry he couldn't have such a long-term "guest," and a week after that they moved into a furnished graduate student apartment on Kenwood that miraculously had just been vacated. "Kismet!" Margaret exclaimed with a delighted smile and threw him on the big double bed and had a wonderful orgasm.

In retrospect she couldn't say if she'd been genuinely happy or just relieved. And she now had to ask herself, what was I so afraid of anyway? What was I after? She remembered quite clearly thinking it would be cool to be a professor's wife (yes, she had said the word "wife" to herself—so unenlightened, as if she were some creature of the 1950s, not the 1990s!). Of course she would matriculate and go to graduate school, too. Anthropology or something. But yes, that was what she wanted. A life with Henry. A life—and a home. A real home. That's what the shrink was probably getting at all these years later. Before her father died, she'd had a real home. And that was stolen from her. Mother, of course, was useless. And Margaret, at fourteen, was supposed to do all the taking care of.

"How could you have?" the shrink told her at least twenty times. "You were only a kid. You have to forgive yourself."

As it turned out, she hated Chicago, hated the town, the weather, the school, and especially all the dweebs at the university who were so socially inept and absurdly intellectual. Not a clue about the real world. Their parties were the worst. You'd see them gather around a wheel of Brie from the Hyde Park Co-op and argue about fucking Heidegger. They were constantly trying to outdo one another in the smarts department. And there was this weird sexual vibe to everything. Like everyone was sleeping with everyone, or wanted to. The professors were particularly egregious with their minions of coeds and adoring acolytes. Gay, straight— it was like being in the middle of a nerd pornfest.

She got a job in the social services library. When that didn't work, she took one as phone operator for the medical center. When that didn't work, she took an art appreciation class at the extension and finally became a teacher's aide at the Lab School. That was a nightmare, but Henry was proud of her. And so the months dragged on and then the years. She never did anything to matriculate. Henry's classes piled one atop the other like the books on his desk, melting into one continuous jargon-filled term paper. He seemed no closer to finishing. The boredom, though, was strangely narcotic. She sat for hours doing nothing. Henry was either in class or at the library or hidden behind a book in his easy chair. She had a few friends, but actually she hated them. They'd have a dinner party and the next day she couldn't remember what they'd eaten. And when they did go out, it was to some lame lecture or a student concert or fucking *folk dancing*. And worst of all, two years had slipped by and he had yet to ask her to marry him.

One day, Henry came home and asked Margaret to sit down next to him on the sofa.

"This is going to be hard," he began.

She braced herself. Where would she go? What would she do?

"I can't do this anymore," he said.

"Henry, please—"

"I don't want to finish my degree."

"What?"

"I know it's terrible. After all I've put you through."

"You don't—"

"Maybe I don't have what it takes, I don't know. But I just don't like it anymore. And the politics—you always have to be on your guard. Everyone's always putting everyone down. I feel so outside, you know? I don't fit."

"Really?" she said, trying to gauge his intent.

"Yeah. It's pretty awful." He sighed. It was perhaps the first time she ever heard him sigh.

"What are we going to do?" she asked.

Now came the second sigh. The second ever.

"You do know what we are going to do, don't you?" she said.

"No. I really don't."

"But you were going to be a professor. We were going to live at a university. We would go to faculty teas and be happy. Remember?"

"I know, I know. I'm so sorry."

She still wasn't sure if she could say what she really thought, so she put her arms around him and said, "I'm so sorry, Henry. I am. This was our dream. Your dream. Did I mess it up for you?"

"You? No! No, never! You are the only good thing in my life. You're great. You're loving and loyal and fun and, Christ, you never complained about any of it."

"I just wanted you to be happy," she said.

"But I'm not. I'm not happy here. I want— I don't know—"

She stroked his hair. Her own heart was pounding. She didn't want him to notice, so she turned ever so slightly away and pressed his head to her shoulder.

"Are you?" he said. "Are you happy here? Because if you are I can make it work. I'll just do it, you know?"

"It doesn't matter what I want," she said. "I just want to know what's next. What are we going to do?"

"I don't know."

"But you *have* to know, Henry."

"It's just all so new. I mean I've been thinking about it for a long time, but—"

"Well then you must have a plan."

"I don't. I don't know where you got the idea that I always know what to do. I never know what to do. I mean, I've been thinking I should quit for over a year!"

A wave of panic went through her and then, as if on the wings of angels, went sailing out of her, past the ugly kitchen, the crappy TV, the lumpy bed, and out the sooty window into the crisp Chicago air. A wonderful, long breath fled her lungs and she felt her whole body relax.

"Well," she said, "I have an idea."

And so they returned to San Francisco. And five months later they were married.

———

"My God!" she cried.

"What?" said Peter.

"Oh!" she said. "Nothing. I don't know why I said that."

"Is it something I did?"

"Oh, no, no. Honestly, I don't know why I said that. It must be the alcohol."

He narrowed his eyes. "Are you feeling we shouldn't be doing this?"

"Of course not!" she said with alarm. "Why? Are you?"

"Not at all," he answered, and immediately motioned to the waitress for the check.

They decided on his car for the drive down the mountain, a silver Mercedes, and she asked him, "Why do you think people jump from the Golden Gate Bridge? I mean, think about it, going down, how horrible that must be, how long it must take. You can't turn around and you can't stop it. It's like when you do something in a dream and you can't undo it. Ugh."

"It's stupid to jump," he said.

"No, but think about it. Imagine yourself falling off that bridge."

"I can't," he said.

"Too scary?"

"No, I just can't."

"That's because you're such a positive person," she said, and kissed him on the cheek.

It took about twenty minutes to wind down the Panoramic Highway through the deep woods and out onto the grassy hills that led to the last outcroppings of rock that guard the shore, but soon enough they pulled into the little town of Stinson Beach. It was usually empty in winter, but the fine weather had brought out hundreds of visitors. Margaret had wanted the whole place to herself and she couldn't hide her disappointment.

"Maybe it would have been better if it had rained," she said.

And indeed, Henry had been going on and on about the drought until she wanted to strangle him if he mentioned shower rationing one more time. But today rain would have been a good thing.

They pulled into the small lot in front of the Sandpiper inn, and Margaret grabbed her little overnight bag from the back seat. She'd packed almost nothing but thought she should have some luggage so as not to be too obvious to the innkeeper, even though she knew they were not the first to come just for the day. They'd booked a cottage overlooking the garden and they made all kinds of delighted exclamations to prove to the desk clerk that it was perfect for their vacation, and then they just stood there in the room, listening to each other breathe.

"Maybe we should close the door," Margaret said.

Peter did as she asked, and Margaret set down her overnight on the easy chair.

Peter looked around and said, "It's a nicer room than I imagined." And then he fell silent.

"Why are you so nervous?" she asked.

"I'm not nervous."

"You seem nervous."

And he said, "I'm *not* nervous."

"I am."

"I guess I am, too," he said.

"It's not like it's our first time."

"No."

"So why are we nervous?"

But she knew.

Because, at least for Margaret, it was indeed like the first time. What she had come to realize on the deck of the Mountain Home Inn was that today she would make love to Peter with the knowledge that this might actually mean something;

that she was stepping away from the life she had built so assiduously with Henry, her husband of thirteen years. Thirteen years and eight months and sixteen days. She wondered why she could remember such detail down to the number of days. She knew that as soon as she touched Peter, as soon as her hands went round his shoulders and her mouth caressed his lips, her life would utterly change. She realized she was trembling, and she didn't know if it was with sexual excitement or fear or what. This was very disconcerting to her, because being in control, being the one in control, was how she liked to define herself. Not that she was a controlling person, no, no, not at all, she was not a controlling person—but she did know herself well enough to recognize that when she was feeling out of control she did strange things, sometimes cruel things and sometimes destructive things, but this time she did nothing. She just stood there trembling.

She wondered what Henry was doing right then. It was almost three in the afternoon. The days were short this time of year and the sun was already beginning to sink in the sky, but he was probably as oblivious to that as he was to everything else—he was in some meeting, she guessed, or sitting at his desk writing a report, or probably just taking a nap or playing one of his stupid video games. Why did he have to daydream so much? Why couldn't he be more like Peter?

Peter stepped over to the picture window to draw the blinds but stopped for a moment to view the beach. She could see beyond him the edge of the water, gray and a bit foreboding, as it broke upon the shore in raucous waves, leaving fine trails of bubbles that sank into the sand or retreated back into the sea. It was almost silent because of the thickness of the glass, but here and there the call of the seagulls broke through, and then the sound of children romping in the surf.

"Kids," Peter mused. "They don't feel a damned thing."

"Sorry?"

"It's freezing. The water's freezing. They're in up to their waists."

"Their parents shouldn't let them."

"Oh, why not? They're made of iron. They'll be fine."

He snapped the blinds shut and turned around to face her.

He was the right kind of man to be a father, strong, easygoing, decisive, and kids are made of iron. He would know exactly what to do. A good father. Although it was obvious he had already put the children out of his mind— if they had made any impression in the first place. Things came into Peter's line of sight and then were gone. No residue. This was an amazing, beautiful thing, because for her, the children's giggles were still hovering in the space between them.

Bones was always going on about having kids. He probably thought she hated kids. She didn't. She just—she always thought she wasn't ready. And now—she was forty-two!

A lot of their crowd had them—one, two, even three little things running around like wild animals. She liked the babies, though. It was fun holding them and doing the coo-coo thing, placing the bottle in their mouths, swaying to comfort them. The way their little lips formed a perfect *O* and their hands squeezed and kneaded her fingers as they drank. It was when they got older that they were intimidating. She didn't quite *get* kids, had no idea what they wanted or what to say to them, and not a few times caused a four-year-old to break into monumental sobs. Which of course mortified her. Everyone told her if she had her own it would come naturally, not to worry. She decided they wanted her to have children to validate what they were doing with their own thwarted lives. But a part of her did believe they were right. She would have made a fine mother. And yet she kept saying *no* to Henry.

It was really only in the last few years she understood.

It was when she landed the job at Regency.

Henry was clearly going nowhere in his job. Whatever had held him back in Chicago was holding him back now and would hold him back forever. But Margaret was filled with hunger, a hunger that had been growing inside her for years but that she'd refused to acknowledge. She had thought of it merely as her "work ethic." You go for broke no matter what. Hadn't her father told her a million times there were no halfways? No matter how small or stupid the job. You always give 100 percent. That was her mantra: you can't live in a half-built house. But she came to see there was something else roiling that heart of hers, and one day it burst out into the open and she had to embrace it even if it embarrassed her to say it—she was after greatness. Yes, greatness. She didn't want to just succeed. She wanted success on the grand scale. She wanted money, freedom, power—she wanted, well, it was the whole world she wanted. When she admitted that this was who she really was, she had that same floating feeling she'd had when she first met Henry, only this time it was real. It was coming from within; it had nothing to do with anyone but herself. Was it selfish? Maybe it was. But when they took her on at Regency and told her they expected great things from her, *great* things, it all suddenly became real. The path was laid out before her. It was almost sexual, her excitement; her body was in flames, her very pores exploded with vitality, her skin glowed, her eyes sparkled, her thighs shivered. She took Henry out to a nightclub and they actually danced (well, she did; he talked).

And a few weeks later she realized she was pregnant.

Jesus! It was the first time they'd done it in, like, five months! And it wasn't as if she was really having sex with *him*—she barely felt his presence—she wanted, rather, to share her mastery, her triumph—not with him, but over him.

But there it was, and she was terrified. This terror was quite unlike anything else she had faced, a terror mixed with joy, a joy she was flabbergasted to feel.

She went into the closet of her bedroom to study herself in the full-length mirror. She was thirty-eight years old. Still ripe. Still decent-looking. Nice boobs. She tried to imagine herself with a fat belly, a huge, round, bulbous, outrageous belly with a giant belly button and whatever else goes along with it—that strange dark line running down the middle. It was crazy, but she found it somehow pleasant, even wonderful. Everyone says being pregnant is beautiful. She never thought so, but maybe she'd been wrong. Ever since she took the test she'd been touching her stomach every two minutes, half to see if it was getting any bigger, but half to see—it blew her mind even to think it—if she could feel the life growing within her. In the mirror, she was still just Margaret. In a couple of weeks, who would she be? She'd already gone online to Rosie Pope and Séraphine to check out the maternity clothes and then over to Tory Burch and Prada because she read that a lot of their stuff works just as well.

All the really successful women had kids. Arianna Huffington had kids. Margaret loved Arianna Huffington. So what was the problem? What *was* the problem?

And then, as if the mirror into which she had been looking suddenly shattered into a thousand shards of sunshine, she saw what she so long had refused to see.

It wasn't that she didn't want kids. It was that she didn't want them with Henry.

―――――

The next few weeks were beyond horrible. At least three times she decided to tell Henry, but something always rose up in her and screamed *NO*. She called Planned Parenthood and the Women's Options Center at UCSF. They were immensely kind and nonjudgmental and incredibly delicate and spoke in soft, consoling voices, all of which sent shivers down her spine. She found herself pacing the hallway of her house or wandering up and down Market Street, talking to herself like a madwoman. She should have been at work, she scolded herself, she should have been able to handle it. But she spent hours in front of the computer reading everything she could about babies and how to raise them, and also everything about abortions and how to deal with one, and also everything about couples therapy and how to have a happy marriage, and also everything about the stages of pregnancy and about Lamaze and about preschool and about divorce.

In the end though, none of it mattered.

About eight weeks in, cramps. She was in the office and tried to hide the fact that she couldn't stand straight as she made her way to the ladies' room. She was hoping it was diarrhea—but it was blood, dark and thick, and some other viscous something that filled the bowl. The intense pain dissipated enough so that she could breathe normally. What does one do when this happens, she asked herself? Miscarriage was the one thing she hadn't read about. In a panic, she wadded some paper towels between her legs and got herself to the elevator. She took a cab to the hospital, the paper towels growing wetter and wetter between her legs. They did a D and C and sent her home.

When Henry arrived that evening he saw she was in bed.

"Why didn't you call?" he said.

"It's just a flu."

"Jesus, Margaret, you look like shit. You should have called. I would have come home earlier."

"Why? I'm fine. I'm fine on my own. I'm always fine on my own."

Margaret never did tell him the truth. Instead, she spent a day or two in bed with the flu, never complaining, though Henry perhaps did not understand why a flu would make her weep so uncontrollably. Especially as he had never seen her cry before in their entire married life.

————

So when exactly had she begun to despise her husband? She really couldn't say anymore. She knew she felt it that time he left the bathroom door open. She felt it when he touched his tongue to his upper lip when he was thinking one of his long-winded thoughts. She felt it every time he touched her or even brushed up against her, every time he flipped the pages of a magazine from back to front instead of from front to back, every time she noticed some of his hairs in the sink or socks on the floor or crumbs from his toast adhering to the front of his shirt. But all this was so silly, so superficial and priggish. And yet these moments did happen. These flashes of repulsion. Not always. Just sometimes. But each was a kind of awakening. A warning. *Despised* was too strong a word. She didn't despise him. The word *contempt* sometimes came into her head, and she tried very hard to dispel it, because she knew what that meant—when couples had contempt for their partners it meant the marriage was over.

But now, at this very moment—in this faraway hotel room with the closed blinds and shut door, and the salty, damp air, and the surf rolling somewhere in the distance, and the tinkling laughter of children in the waves, and the blond man standing by the window—the sad truth dawned on her. She could no longer suppress words like "contempt" or hide from other words like "despair," or put her hopes into some lockbox and make believe there were no regrets. Her face revealed nothing and her voice was the same as before, but it really wasn't until this very second she admitted she was ready to end her marriage to Henry.

Peter let go of the blinds. He stepped toward her and took her hands in his, roughly, like he was crushing two walnuts. When Henry took her hands it was more like he was holding two wafers at Communion. She could see that Peter was pleased that she was trembling, and he drew her to him so forcefully her breasts smashed upon his chest, and when he pinned her hands behind her back their bodies were touching from head to toe and there was no space between them, no space at all, and for a moment she couldn't breathe, but then he released her hands and slid his palms down onto her hips, her thighs.

To be taken by such a man as this! So alive, so vital. His eyes were so blue, so full of steel, and his hair so blond, like a laurel of gold.

She wanted to be inside this man, inside this moment.

But she couldn't help pulling back just a little.

She knew he was going through a nasty divorce and that he was currently living in a rented apartment with hardly any furniture in it, and that his wife had the house, and that she wasn't quite sure what he did for a living, and that somewhere he had two children, but he hardly mentioned them. This concerned her: the fact that she'd never met his children, because why was he shielding them from her?

Of course she was being absurd—how would he introduce her to his children? Kids, this is my lover, Margaret, who is also married, by the way, and, no, your mother and I are never getting back together because as you can see, I prefer Margaret to her by a long shot, so go ahead, give her a big hug!

Crazy.

But it was all about the children, wasn't it? All about the children.

His lips were but a millimeter from her own, and his hands were cupping her buttocks and his fingers were groping the space between them and she felt him ratchet up the hem of her skirt and then the galvanizing roughness of his right hand on her left thigh sent a pulse through her entire body, and she cried out, "Peter, I have to meet your kids!"

"What?" he said.

"What?" she replied.

"What did you say?"

"Did I say something?"

"You asked about my kids."

"I did?"

"For Christ's sake, Margaret, what's with you today?"

"No, no!" she said. "Don't move away! Stay. Keep doing what you were doing."

"Margaret, sit down. We need to talk."

"No, no, I don't want to talk!"

"Well, I do," he said. "You sound so—"

"I'm not neurotic!" she cried. "I'm the least neurotic person I know!"

"I didn't say you were neurotic. For Christ's sake, just sit down!"

She collapsed beside him on the edge of the bed. Immediately she noticed the mattress was too firm for her, but she ordered herself not to say anything about it, to let it go.

"Margaret," he said, "what's going on with you?"

"This bed is too hard," she said.

"It's not the bed that's too hard for you. You're having second thoughts, aren't you? "

"No, it's just the bed."

"It's all this subterfuge. Maybe you just can't do this anymore."

She noticed her fists had hardened into little balls, and she snarled, "Are you talking about me or are you talking about you?"

"Why must you deflect everything?"

"I'm not deflecting anything. Did I say I'm having second thoughts? Did I say it's too hard for me?"

"No, you didn't."

"So why are you attacking me?"

"I'm not attacking you, Margaret."

"Then why do I feel attacked? The fucking bed is too hard. It's bad for your back."

Peter sighed and looked away.

"Oh Jesus, Peter, come back," she cried. "I'm just, I don't know. It was the bridge. It was that woman, or girl, or whatever she was. Can't you understand it upset me? Wouldn't you be upset, seeing someone jump off the Golden Gate Bridge?"

"She didn't jump," said Peter.

Margaret slapped herself. "Oh shit!" she cried. "I forgot completely. I left it in the fucking car."

"What did you leave? I'll get it for you."

"No," she said, "in the MINI Cooper. My Christmas present for you. I have this present I want to give you." Suddenly she was weeping, just weeping, and it was crazy because what was the big deal? "From Tiffany's," she cried.

"It's all right," he said. "Honestly. I don't need a gift. I have you." And she knew at that moment that he hadn't bought her anything for Christmas. She felt a little ridiculous, because, of course, presents are superfluous if you have love.

"You're right," she said. "I didn't see anyone jump. But I could imagine it. I could feel what it was like. You know what I mean?"

"Not really."

Only now did he stand up and, without a word, pulled her into his arms. His face loomed above her, the mop of blond hair framing his pale blue eyes, the tan skin glowing even in winter, the slight pudginess of his cheeks and neck bespeaking health and the kind of imperviousness that comes with being one of the owners of the world, and not, like Henry, a mere observer. She glanced down at his hands and at his school ring and on his other hand the mark where his wedding band used to be, and then up to the tie he was wearing—a tie even on a day of trysting—as usual it hung slightly askew from his collar. She took note of his lips, which she always thought of as sweet but in fact were firm and hard, and then she dared to stare back into his eyes, which were so intensely focused on the pleasure he was about to experience.

"You don't think about all that much, do you?" she said.

"I guess not," he said.

"I'm glad," she said. "I really am."

And with that he began to methodically unbutton her blouse with his practiced hand, one button and then another and another, and she knew with absolute certainty that each button opened was a step she was taking off the edge of her own Golden Gate Bridge, and that when no buttons were left and her breasts were exposed to his callused hands, she would have already leapt beyond the railings, and in her falling she would be filled with regret, but also exultation, and for once in her life she would be flying without ropes, without a net, and without ever again having the chance to go home.

PART THREE

DAISY

CHAPTER 9

December 23rd, 2:24–2:35 p.m.

What exactly was in Daisy's mind we don't know, only that she uttered aloud, "Daisy, Daisy, Daisy, Daisy, you ninny, you idiot." No doubt she wished she could compress herself into the size of an atom or a molecule like one of her retinal neurons and disappear into the glop of some cosmic eyeball, but in fact she waited (and waited) for Henry in front of SlinkyBlink thinking, or hoping at least, that he would follow her, and when after an interminable five minutes he hadn't, she felt herself grow slightly hysterical and had to remind herself that he needed to pay the bill and that takes time, but after another five minutes and then another, that battle was lost: she burst into tears. People on the street began staring at her, and one young woman even came up to her and offered to call a cab. This was so humiliating she couldn't even manage a thank-you and instead ran off in the direction of the garage, up the Sutter Street hill. Get it together, she scolded herself. But the tears still burned in her eyes and the stifled sobs constricted her throat and made it hard to breathe. She was standing at the pay station when out of the corner of her eye she saw him—Henry passing the entrance to the garage—and by some perverse instinct hid herself behind the ticket machine. Only when she was sure he had gone did she step out onto the street to watch him disappear past the Starbucks on the corner. She didn't call out, didn't run after him. She did take out her hanky and blow her nose. Then she went back inside, put her money in the ticket machine, and made her way to her car.

Daisy had moved all the way out to Fairfax in Marin County several years before, so she had a long drive, which would at least give her time to think, but it was not thought that filled her, it was desire: not carnal desire, but desire of the soul—she wanted what she had once possessed but had discarded like old wrapping paper. She wanted her companion; she wanted peace; she wanted laughter in her bed and passion in her veins. She wanted Bones—her dear, beautiful Bones, her funny, silly, brilliant, impossibly possible

Bones. When you lose something, she thought, you can't have it back just because you want it. You have to accept loss. That's what Bones was always telling her about Buddha. You can't hold on. You can't become attached. But all these years had passed and she had not accepted.

What a selfish bitch I am! she thought. She was so upset she pressed too hard on the gas and had to swerve to avoid some prostitute on the corner of Pine and Mason—well, she looked like a prostitute—and suddenly Daisy was filled with jealousy. That prostitute is so damned lucky, Daisy thought. She doesn't need love. She just needs fifty bucks. And then she got angry at herself for thinking this. Prostitutes have feelings, too. It's not their fault. Something horrible happened to them. Something horrible some man did. A father. A brother. A pimp.

But Henry hadn't done anything wrong. He hadn't taken anything from her. He'd given. And now he lived inside her in ways she could not have anticipated that terrible night when she ordered him out of her life. Out of her life! What a joke. She had been so appalled at his lack of contrition. But really what he meant was that his love was greater than some stupid, moribund convention and the life he offered her was so full of truth and fire that everything else was a lie.

The day she broke up with Henry was a Thursday. She remembered this because *Glee* was on that night and they used to watch it together over the phone when Edward wasn't home and she had just the kids—she would call him "Sally" so her children wouldn't guess she was speaking to a man. A lot of men did not like *Glee*, but Henry liked *Glee*. When she'd asked Edward to watch with her he'd say, "So gay!" and go back to whatever it was he was doing that wasn't quite so gay. Frankly, she couldn't imagine Margaret watching it, either. Of course, she barely knew Margaret. They had met at a function or two for BrainPower for Kids when Margaret had accompanied Henry. She was quite— let's say—*erect*, with sharp hips pointed at whomever she was speaking with. Her hair was incredibly glowy and smooth, cut in a severely angled bob. Elegant and intimidating, at least to Daisy. Not to mention the boarding-school savior faire about her, a frisson of noblesse oblige that was evident in the way she twisted her right foot on its stiletto heel as she spoke. Daisy had to remind herself over and over that Margaret sold fucking real estate and Daisy was the one with all the money.

She wasn't even supposed to break up with him that Thursday. It just sort of happened. Earlier that afternoon they'd met in Sausalito, as they so often had. It was a sunny and cloudless afternoon, which Bones remarked upon because it had been so cold and foggy in the city and he was delighted to be in the sunshine. She wore her cutoffs and a little halter because, she said, it was so damn hot. It really wasn't that hot and she knew it, so why, on that day, did she wear that outfit?

"Let's go inside," she said, pointing to the café on the square.

"No, no, let's enjoy the weather."

"I want to go inside," she insisted.

"But why?"

"Because it's too public out here."

"Who cares if someone sees us?" he said. "We're just talking."

But she knew he would try to kiss her—he always did. She would put him off with a playful shove and then he would throw his arm around her waist thinking it very surreptitious, but they both knew it wasn't: it was dangerous—and something in him liked danger. *Henry Danger, private dick*, that's what she secretly called him. But today, she didn't want to risk it.

She found herself throwing off his hand and quickening her pace. The square was teeming with tourists—moms, dads, kids, young honeymooners. Families, she thought. All these families. The other night she'd asked him—don't you feel any remorse? How can you not care about other people's feelings? It had been working on her for days, actually. Where was his moral compass? Where was hers?

She jogged over to the café and found a table off to the side even though he wanted to sit by the window.

"What are you going to have?" he asked.

"Nothing."

"Not hungry?"

"No. You can eat if you want to."

"You should eat."

"I don't want to eat."

"Then why are we in a restaurant?"

"It's not a restaurant. It's a coffee place."

"Then have some coffee."

"Jesus, what are you, Mother Teresa? Stop it!"

That's of course when he started stuttering. He always stuttered when people yelled at him. Not exactly a stutter, more like sleep apnea only awake. Gagging. Gasping.

"Can you stop that?" she said.

"Sto-sto- wha-wha-?"

"Stuttering. Stop stuttering."

"I don't st-st—"

"If you don't breathe you're going to faint, for God's sake. Calm down."

"I'm sorry," he said. "Whatever I did—"

"It's okay. It's okay. I'm just cranky. I think you're right, I need something to eat."

He smiled. "Hypoglycemia, I've seen it before."

"Have you?" she said.

"Many times. I'll get you a *pain au chocolat*. It's a sure cure."

"Fine," she said, watching him go. Instinctively she went for her lipstick, then decided against it. Instead, she adjusted her shorts, tried to stretch the bottom of the halter to cover a little more of her tummy. He came back with the croissant, a couple of cappuccinos, some napkins, and a banana.

"Banana is, like, the best for hypoglycemia," he crowed. "Plus very, very delicious with chocolate."

"Stop being so nice to me," she said, sensing that something had already moved within her, a tectonic shift deep within the substratum of her soul. It was all those families. All those children and husbands and wives. Her family. His family. Her heart went out to Margaret, who was the innocent one here, in the dark completely. What on earth had Henry and she been thinking?

This was the moment in which she'd at last made up her mind. It had to stop. Love had nothing to do with it, she told herself. Love was just a feeling. Not important. Not like family. It's just she couldn't find the words to tell him. Not when he was offering her a chocolate croissant and a banana.

She took a deep breath, searched her mind for an answer and then told him that, as Edward would be away that evening, would he like to come by after the kids were asleep?

"Really?" he said.

"Yes. Please."

"Then you're not mad at me?"

"No, I'm not mad."

"We can watch *Glee*."

"After *Glee,* Henry. After the kids are asleep."

———

Exactly an hour after *Glee,* there was his knock on the door. She suspected he'd been waiting in the car, checking his watch, not wanting to intrude on her kid time, but impatient and excited to see her nonetheless. He was sweet that way. Considerate. Always putting her first. Hanging on her words as if they were droplets of gold. Actually listening. But she had already decided she would not ask him in. Because if she did . . . He knocked again. She grasped the knob but found she could not turn it. He knocked again. That knock reverberated all the way down to her toes. What choice did she have? She opened the door. He smiled—even in the dark of night there was sunshine all over his face— and took a step forward. Instantly she placed her hand on his chest to stop him.

"Let's go outside," she said. "The kids."

"I thought they were asleep."

"What if they wake up?"

She led him onto the front deck and down the stairs to the lawn. The air was thick with redwood and jasmine, still warm from the day's heat, the sky a clear lens through which the star-filled heavens shimmered.

"It's nice out here, too," he said.

She tried like hell to remember what she'd rehearsed— nothing came into her head.

"I can't see you anymore, Henry!" she finally blurted. "I apologize, I do."

"Really? I can still see you. The moon's out. But I can get a flashlight if you want."

"No, Henry. No. You're not hearing me. I can't do *this* anymore."

"This?"

"*Us.*"

His throat caught, but he managed to squeak, "Are you serious?"

"It's not right, Bones. It's just not right. And you of all people should know that. You're a good person, Henry. I believe that. But this—no. Please just go home!" she said, or something to that effect because by now she couldn't remember the exact words, but she clearly did see herself turning tail and running into the house, that gigantic house, before he had a chance to respond. Whatever he was going to say, she didn't want to hear it, couldn't hear it, wouldn't hear it. She slammed the door behind her. Perhaps not really *slammed*. She wouldn't do that. Especially with the kids asleep. But it might as well have been a slam. She pressed her back upon it, though, to make sure it was shut—and waited for him to run up and knock, pound, cry. But he didn't. This surprised her. And when she heard the car starting and the spinning of tires on the gravel drive and the crunching of gears furiously thrown into forward, and finally the fading, fading, fading of the engine as he drove off into oblivion, that thing inside her that had sent him away now became rather frightened, and maybe a little angry. Everything was so quiet. The house. The yard. The dog. The children. She felt incredibly alone.

But then something occurred to her. She was . . . free. Free from all the lies and deceit. Free to feel at home again. The noise of all that love was behind her now, far, far down that road. Everything would be as it was. The air would be clear again. The sky would go back to being just sky. The mirror could once again reflect the woman her husband married.

She wandered a few minutes through the house, running her fingers over the edge of the couch, the porcelain statuettes, the lid of the Steinway; she looked with fresh eyes at the paintings on the walls and the photographs on the mantel; she passed through the living room, the library, the gallery, and ended up where she and Edward and the kids had spent so many hours together—Edward's home theater. It might as well have been an IMAX with its acoustically tuned walls specially made to look like zebrawood, three rows of deluxe stadium seating with their rosewood armrests, the massive 3-D screen with speakers practically everywhere, including under your feet and in the headrests of your seat. In one corner there was even a popcorn machine. Edward's world.

Ridiculous and pretentious! But now she wondered if she had judged him too harshly. There was some sweetness here, too, wasn't there? She sunk into one of Edward's seats. The lush vicuna inlay on the armrests comforted her and the closeness of the room calmed her. Daisy pondered the screen upon which, just an hour ago, she and her children had watched the latest episode of *Glee*, laughing and singing along with the cast. It was fun. It was healthy and honest and clean and normal. Now, of course, the screen was dark, a just-washed blackboard on a schoolroom wall. Or a black hole, like outer space. A wonderful emptiness, quietude, serenity. She let forth a long, languorous exhalation—all the tension, all the secrets, all the convolutions, all the excuses and deceptions, the wishing she was elsewhere, the wishing she were someone else—all of it went out of her.

She closed her eyes. She heard the silence all about. She hugged herself tightly. She felt herself go slightly faint. She already knew that everything she had been telling herself was a lie.

CHAPTER 10

3:01–3:25 p.m.

So, yeah, Daisy now told herself as she drove back to Marin, she'd thrown Henry out, and so what? In his absence he became more powerful than ever, and he stood within her as a guide and confidante, explaining her own life to her, counseling her in her moments of doubt and assuring her that her future was her own to grasp; that she could leave her husband, go back to school and still raise her kids; that somehow they wouldn't starve and the world wouldn't fall apart; and when she went looking for boyfriends he showed her they weren't enough, didn't know a thing about her, hadn't a clue what a real relationship should be. In short, no one else knew how to love her.

Because it wasn't really his lack of remorse that had upset her so much that day. It was her own.

And so when she saw him standing in front of Slinky-Blink after all those years apart, and he was exactly the same as she remembered him, still lost in some crazy Henry stream of thought, staring into the window of a store in which he would never set foot, allowing his mind to wander wherever it might, and when she also realized that he had gained only a few pounds and that the khakis he wore were the very ones they had purchased together that day at Banana Republic, she was suddenly incapable of anything but striding up to him and saying hello. She had organized her best smile and most practiced air of insouciance, and even though she profoundly desired to come up behind him and wrap her arms around him the way she used to do, she merely tapped him on the shoulder and gently called out his name, saying it aloud for the first time in four years.

What had she thought would happen? That he would gather her in his arms and carry her off to the South of France? Maybe she had. Yes, she had. But then he said he loved Margaret.

He meant it, too.

And yet didn't he seem to look for her in the garage as he passed by?

She was now already approaching the span of the Golden Gate Bridge. She was a little concerned because she had to pick up Tasha at school and she'd heard there had been some snafu at the bridge, but she could now see the traffic was flowing smoothly. Apparently someone had decided to jump. Of course. It's Christmas. Later they said it might have been a motorcycle accident or a pedestrian who fell into the traffic lane or maybe there *was* a jumper but they talked the guy down. She hadn't really been listening. She had decided to concentrate on work instead of Henry, and the radio just became noise, like a foreign language. She'd been trying to create a kinetic model of photo transduction that included a detailed stochastic simulation of the activation and inactivation of rhodopsin, G-protein, and phosphodiesterase. Well, it wasn't her project exactly: it was her lab's, her teacher and adviser Dr. Russell's; she was merely a helper bee. But it was clear he was steering her dissertation in this direction and it was disheartening because so far they had gotten pretty much nowhere. It so happened it was quite challenging to create a mathematical equation that accurately described the molecular path of a single receptor cell as it responded to a particular wavelength of light. And now she tried to figure out why it wasn't working. That would be a good thing to concentrate on, she thought. She knew that the rhodopsin molecule underwent a series of phosphorylation steps and that each sequential step led to a progressive decrease in affinity between rhodopsin and the G-protein, and concomitantly to a progressive increase in affinity between R and Arr, and that the affinity between R and RK also ratchets down and—here her mental acuity failed her. Not because she couldn't handle the R's and RK's and whatnot, but because she couldn't get out of her mind the fact that he was still so cute, the jerk. He hadn't changed, not an iota. Not a tittle, not a tot! How could someone still be so attractive after all that time? So adorable. So, so . . . she found herself at a total loss for words.

The guy wore his heart so far out on his sleeve it was on the next block. It was nuts. He was nuts. She was nuts. After all, she had been with men, real men, and he was more like a little boy sometimes. But she knew that really wasn't so. There was no word for who he was! He was a good guy, a very good guy, a guy with soul, with tenderness. And that beautiful brain of his that never stopped!

How could he love Margaret?

Daisy truly didn't want to think negative thoughts about Margaret, but they came anyway because she was certain that Margaret was unfaithful and mean-spirited, at least when it came to Henry. Why wouldn't she have children? Because she was selfish, that's why. She was the opposite of Henry; she was his evil doppelgänger. No, doppelgänger is the same, a carbon copy. She was nothing like him. No one was.

I would have kids with him, she thought.

And why not? She was only thirty-eight. They could have two! And the children they'd make together would be amazing and beautiful, because these would be the children of love, the children of *true* love. And Tasha and Denny would love them, too. How could they not? Especially Denny, because he would be the big brother who would take care of them, and Tasha always said she wanted a sister anyway, and then Tasha and Denny would also have Bones to help them and love them and be a father to them. Tasha and Denny would totally love Bones back; they would adore him because he'd be more of a father than their own father, because Edward was more like an absentee landlord with them. And the new kids—Allison and Alex—they'd go to Marin Country Day, too, which was where she was headed at this very moment to pick up Tasha. She didn't have to worry about Denny today, he had basketball over at Marin Academy. They were already letting him practice with the freshman squad—that's how good he was—and he was also going to be on the ski team, he hoped. So she just had Tasha, and all she had to do was drop Tasha at Marin Ballet for her level-four class, which Tasha was beginning to lose interest in, which would be a shame.

So Daisy starting thinking how she could keep Tasha in dancing, and she decided maybe she could discuss it with the teacher, today if possible, because Tasha had been dancing five years already, no six, since pre-ballet in kindergarten. You had to give it to Edward, he never held the money over their heads, not once; he just paid, and paid happily, and you never even had to ask him. So in that way, yes, he was a good father, and a swath of warmth for Edward came over her as she exited 101 toward Paradise Drive, because people can only show their love in ways that are natural to them, and that was his way, and it wasn't the worst possible way, it simply wasn't a way that fed her soul. That was a different path, a path of love, the one Bones had shown her. If only she had had the eyes to see it.

No, that wasn't true.

She *had* seen it. And it had terrified her.

She should have just shut her eyes and followed him to the edge and jumped. Jump, jump, jump! What an idiot she was! she told herself.

But she'd let him go and that was the end of it. When you lose something you don't get it back. That's the law of karma he'd tried to show her.

It was like that problem she and Bones were always arguing about. If Daisy were standing on the front of a freight train, holding a flashlight, and Bones were standing on the front of another freight train facing her, also holding a flashlight, and both trains were heading toward each other at, say, five hundred miles per hour, then each of them should see light coming toward them at the speed of light plus one thousand miles per hour, which is his train speed plus her train speed plus the speed of light. But no. No matter how fast the trains are heading toward each other, the light takes exactly C, the speed of light—no matter how you measure it, either from a standing position or a moving position, from the front, from the side, from above or from below, from on the train or off the train, from near or from far. The speed of light is absolute, and there is nothing you can do about it. No alterations allowed. This was the conundrum—illogical, impossible, but unassailably true—in which she found her whole life mired. The speed of love was fixed. Her movement toward Henry Quantum was unchangeable, just as his movement away from her was. The immutable law of loss insisted they would never reach

each other, no matter how hard she tried, no matter how fast she ran, no matter how much love she emitted. Their lights would never collide.

She now was within sight of the Village shopping center, which was packed with shoppers and ablaze with Christmas lights even though the sun was still out. She turned right onto Paradise Drive, which wound along the lip of the cove like a hawk circling a field, but it was a route that always gave her a sense of peace, perhaps because she knew her daughter was waiting at the end of it. But today she let her foot off the gas because she was in no hurry to get there, they'd make her wait in line at the roundabout anyway, but also she wanted to be alone with her thoughts, to have a little more time to think them, because she hadn't come to the heart of it yet, to the part in which she could see her way through all the tumult of feelings to whatever lay within.

And so she pulled over to the side of the road just a few yards up from the police station. She knew other parents would pass her, perhaps even recognize her, but she didn't care. She simply wasn't ready for the onslaught of Tasha and all her demands and complaints and the begging not to go to ballet. It was the last day of school before Christmas holiday and that would add to the craziness, with all the kids bringing home their art portfolios and science projects and all the other things they were done with now that the semester was over. Everyone was still going on about the winter concert and the fifth-grade show and how hard their exams were, and the energy would be frenetic, and Daisy needed a bit of quiet. She turned off the engine and released her grip on the steering wheel. She removed her phone from her purse and placed it on her lap.

She looked at that phone for a very long time.

Don't make a fool of yourself, she said silently.

Not everyone appreciated Henry, she knew that. On paper Edward was far his superior: Aside from the fact that Edward came from money and was uniquely able to make more and more money as if there was nothing to it, Edward was, well, he was beautiful, by which she meant he was much more than handsome—he was gorgeous, electrifying, like a movie star—and women were drawn to him in droves. She knew he slept with a lot of them, too, and for the longest time she accepted this as the price of being married to such a man: the price for in-laws with a house in Napa and another in the Hamptons, a main residence in Ross and a pied-à-terre on Russian Hill; the price for the extravagant and interesting parties with the Gettys and the Betzes and the Hellmans; for the eighteen-foot Christmas trees and the buffet breakfasts served by staff; for the family cruises and the family horses and the family "getaways" on Kauai and in Aix and Fiesole and on the private island off Bali; for the opening-night box at the opera and the easy reservations at French Laundry; for the satisfaction of donating large sums and seeing your largess do good in the world; for the privilege of hanging on his arm in public and becoming more desirable because of it. The price for all this, unfortunately, was Edward. His unthinking infidelities. His unfailing denseness. His unholy sense of ownership.

She was only twenty-one when he'd scooped her up and married her, only twenty-four when she'd had Denny. Too young, she told herself. Much, much too young.

And then one day it all changed.

"Are you crazy?" he said to her.

He told her he didn't care about her affair with that ad guy, he'd get over it. It wasn't that big a deal.

"It should be a big deal!" she said to him.

"But it's not. Things happen."

"I'm moving out," she screamed. "I'm going back to school. I want to be a scientist. A biologist."

"But why?" he said.

"Because I've always wanted to."

"You always wanted to leave me?"

"I always wanted to be a scientist."

"Daisy, I hate to tell you, you're thirty-four years old. You have two children. They happen to need you; maybe you've forgotten that. And the household and all your volunteer work. And me. I need you. Not that you care about me."

"You'll be fine," she said.

"Daisy, do you have any idea how hard it is in graduate school? You think you can manage that? Be realistic. You don't have a scientific brain, Daisy. You're all over the map. You're terrible at math. What kind of scientist would you be? You'll end up a lab technician. Get a grip. You're having a midlife crisis, that's all." And then to make her feel better he added, "Listen, I've had affairs, too."

"Fuck you," she said.

Until that moment perhaps she had doubted her resolve, but now there was no turning back. She found a little house much farther out in Marin, in Fairfax, in the flats, not much more than a bungalow with a little yard, three small bedrooms, a tiny eat-in kitchen, and a miniscule living room. It was far, far away from the house in Belvedere and felt like a place where you could start over. Fairfax, with its head shops and unrepentant hippies in tie-dyed T-shirts and long floral dresses, was something out of the sixties. Everyone seemed to drive a beat-up Datsun and there was a postbox-size ice-cream shop on Main Street and a real five-and-dime. Daisy felt strangely at home in this retrograde universe and sensed she was returning to something she had long forgotten, though she was much too young to remember the sixties and in reality she was simply a divorced woman with two kids and this is what she could afford. But she enrolled in community college, beefed up her math, took her GRE, and ended up at San Francisco State with an internship at the Hamer Eye Research Institute. She worked part-time in the bookstore in Fairfax until she got a teaching assistantship, and took money from Edward only for the kids' school and their share of the rent, and for nothing else.

When her friends came to visit, they all said to her, "You're crazy."

———

Daisy sat in her car on the shoulder of Paradise Drive thinking about all this and hoping somehow to get to the heart of it, but somehow she wasn't. She decided it was time to concentrate.

How had she met this Henry Quantum? At a meeting of the PR committee of BrainPower for Kids. Someone on the board knew someone at some ad agency who agreed to take them on pro bono. Everyone had been quite excited about it, so they all got there early, which almost never happened, but the agency people arrived late anyway. In came a young woman of indeterminate age and sexual orientation and a lanky guy in his midthirties who seemed to trip over his own feet, which at the time were encased in red high-top sneakers—a strange contrast to the rather conservative suit and club tie he was also wearing. Everyone assumed that he was the art director because of the sneakers and the fact that he kind of looked like some movie or rock star they couldn't place—Justin Bieber? (Only pastier, if that was possible.) Daisy rather thought he looked more like a goofy Ben Affleck. In any event, the guy turned out to be the account manager, so everyone expected him to say slick, annoying account executive things. Except everything he said made sense. He explained things simply, from beginning to end, without making you feel stupid. By the end of the meeting everyone trusted him and unanimously decided to go with whatever the agency said. "Great!" the account guy said, and suggested it would be most efficient if they appointed just one person from the committee to work closely with the agency. Daisy raised her hand and said, "I'll be the liaison on this."

Which surprised everyone because Daisy never volun-
teered for extra duty.

She remembered specifically how her hand felt raised
above her head, her fingers spread wide and wagging about
like little puppy-dog tails. She also remembered how quickly
she put her hand down because she was worried there might
be sweat under her arm.

This, she now knew, is how the universe conspires for
love.

It conspires to teach you something. Only you have to
be willing to learn. It conspires to take you to undiscovered
countries. Only you have to stay the course.

Over coffee at Peet's and over lunch at the Depot and on
the phone at all hours and at his office in the mornings and
at her house on gray afternoons they conspired. They told
themselves their objective was a public persona for Brain-
Power, a way to raise awareness and money, but their course
of action was a conversation that ranged from childhood
reminiscence to political meandering to complaints about
spouses to revealing secret writings kept in drawers to "tell
me what you think this dream means" and "you crack me up
you're so funny" and "I wish I'd met you years ago." They
had more and more of these meetings as the weeks went by,
and less and less progress on the ad campaign. Then one day

Henry traveled to Chicago to shoot a commercial for one of his clients, and that afternoon he called her from O'Hare and said to her:

"Hi, Daisy, I'm just calling to say hello."

"Hello, you," she said.

He took a breath and said, "I know it's crazy, but I miss you."

It seemed forever before she said, "I miss you, too."

"So you know?"

She said, "Yes, I know. I feel the same."

"You do?"

"Yes. I do."

Her heart was pounding, really pounding, and the phone in her hand seemed to shake of its own accord.

He said, "I've never—"

"Me neither," she said.

"It's overwhelming."

"I know."

"But, Daisy—"

"You don't have to say it."

"I do. I have to. We can't let this go anywhere. You know that."

"I do know that."

"It has to stop here. Just with our knowing."

"I know that, Henry."

"We can't let it go any further."

"I agree."

"So this is hello and good-bye."

"Yes," she said with a sigh. "I think so."

There was another pause, this one filled in equal measure with rapture and wretchedness. And when the silence simply became too much, he said, "Hello, Daisy."

She answered, "Hello, Henry."

And then he said, "Good-bye, Daisy."

And she answered, "Good-bye, Henry."

"I'm glad," he said.

"I'm glad, too," she answered.

And honestly they did try not to take it any further. When Henry got back he didn't call her. He went straight home to his wife and told her he had been exhausted from the trip—the 6:00 a.m. production calls, not wrapping till eight, the crew dinners and the barhopping with clients, all the various headaches of trying to please everyone and at the same time keeping a handle on things back at the office, and then the long, horrible flight—the weather was awful! But the truth was the only thing on his mind was Daisy, day and night. It was exhausting! And when he got home all he wanted to do was sleep.

But Margaret needed him to run errands for her and she screamed at him, "Why don't you ever take care of me? Why do you even bother coming home if you're not going to pay attention to me?" He told her he hadn't slept in two days, but she kept waking him up, saying, "I need you to do this for me *now*," and "Why can't I ever count on you?" until finally he just locked himself in the bathroom and went to sleep in the tub, even with her banging on the door, that's how tired he was. It was only then, he'd told Daisy later, that he realized that Margaret didn't actually love him. She merely needed him like you need a handyman or a psychiatrist; when she didn't need him for something, she didn't seem to even notice him. My God, he said to himself lying in the tub, *she's not a wife, she's a client!* It was something any of his friends could have told him years before, but that's Henry.

Two days later he called Daisy and asked her to meet him in the parking lot along the water's edge at Marina Green. When he saw her drive up, he motioned to her and she got into his car and before she could say a word he had enveloped her with kisses; and she kissed him back, felt her entire self kiss him, as if a vise around her heart had suddenly given way, and from her mouth molten kisses erupted from an unexpected fire at her core.

He reached beneath her sweater and touched her nipple. She swooned and it amazed her because she never thought her nipples were sensitive—but they were, they were! There were people about, families strolling up the path along the shoreline or playing on the green behind them. Anyone could see them through the windshield. She didn't care. She wanted to tear off her sweater then and there, but he stopped her by placing two fingers upon her lips and saying, "Shhhh, shhhh. We have all the time in the world."

And at first it seemed they did. Each time they slept together she marked it in her calendar with a smiley face, although she soon changed that to the letter "H" for happiness, because a smiley face could raise suspicions if someone got hold of her phone or looked on her computer. She laughed remembering how she had warned him that first time that she didn't always have orgasms and never, ever, had a multiple one, and then went on to have four that afternoon, four in a single instance, and then more later. It was stunning, and even more so when Henry said, "I didn't do that; you did." But it was only later that she came to know that it was true: it was she herself, in her radical openness, in her openness to him. And now, sitting in the car by the side of the road two days before Christmas, she finally understood she had loved him not for what he did for her but for what he allowed her to do for herself; and that was the core of it, that's what that fire was, that is what she wanted back, and that is what she had lost forever.

Alone in her car by the side of the road, Daisy buried her head between her hands and began to cry.

CHAPTER 11

3:26–4:30 p.m.

Suddenly there was loud knock on the driver's side window and Daisy jumped so hard the seat belt locked and crushed her shoulder. It was a cop.

She cursed herself and rolled down the window.

He leaned in and said, "Everything all right?"

"Oh! Yes, yes."

As she was saying this, her cell phone starting ringing. She wanted to answer it, knew she better not. Knew she had to keep her eyes fixed on the policeman. It was driving her crazy that she couldn't look at the phone to see who was calling.

"You're in a no-stopping zone," he said.

"I am? Oh my gosh, I'm sorry. I just pulled over to think for a minute."

She stole a glance at the phone.

"You need to turn that ringer off, ma'am."

"But I—"

"Please turn the ringer off."

She fumbled for the button and the ringer fell silent.

"Thank you, ma'am," said the officer. "You know it's a sixty-dollar fine."

"I didn't realize I couldn't pull over here, officer. Honest."

"There's the sign right in front of you."

"Oh, gosh, I didn't see it. I'm so sorry."

"You need to pay attention to signs."

"Absolutely. I'm so sorry."

"That's why we have signs. So you pay attention to them."

"Yes, yes!" she cried. "That's the whole problem!" And with that she burst into tears again.

"Ma'am," he said.

"I never see the signs!" She reached out the window and grabbed the policeman's hand. "He used to bring me teddy bears!" she sobbed. "He even named them!"

"Ma'am, have you been drinking?"

"No," she said between sobs, "just half a glass of rosé. We always drank rosé. I drank the rosé," she corrected herself, "he drank Pouilly-Fumé."

"Maybe you should calm down," he said.

"But he was perfect!"

"Nobody's perfect," the policeman said.

"You don't know Bones."

"I don't know what?"

"Bones. That's what everyone calls him. He's skinny. He likes *Star Trek*. Do you have a tissue?"

"No, ma'am."

"I think I have one somewhere. Hold on." She fished through her purse and found a little packet of Puffs and blew her nose.

"Are you all right now, ma'am?"

"Yes. Go on with your ticket. It's okay."

"You know you could have caused an accident. Coming round that curve, other vehicles cannot see you."

"I'm a terrible person," she said.

"You're not a terrible person. You're just illegally parked."

"You're being very nice, Officer. I appreciate it. I do."

She blew her nose again. He rocked back and forth on his heels, waiting for her to finish.

"Okay," he said. "Look, it's almost Christmas. I'm going to let you off with a warning this time."

"Really?" she said.

He scanned the interior of the car for a moment and then did the same to Daisy. "Yes. But you sure you are all right now? I'm taking you at your word that you only had half a glass."

"I'm fine, honestly. I'm fine."

"All right, then. Go ahead and move the vehicle."

"Thank you, Officer."

"Merry Christmas," he said.

And so, gathering her wits as best she could, Daisy engaged the turn signal and gingerly pulled out onto the road. By the time she got to Marin Country Day she was more or less back to normal, normal enough for Tasha at least not to notice, or at least she hoped so. By now she had completely forgotten that her phone had been ringing, and all she wanted was to throw Tasha in the back seat and get her the hell to ballet.

———

But it was not Henry Quantum who had been calling Daisy at that moment, though she had hoped it was. Henry at that hour was still engaged with Santa Claus on the bench in Union Square. It was only Ashiyana Malleshawari calling from India to inquire about a phone bill that had not been paid, because Daisy had thrown it in a pile with other mail and had forgotten all about it, which happened to her frequently, just as she ignored all the text messages and e-mails from AT&T. It was one of the things she never really got used to, paying bills— the accountant had always taken care of them—and at times Edward scolded her about it. The utilities for instance— the electricity came perilously close to being shut off, until Daisy actually read the note banded in red that warned her of the imminent cutoff. And there were also the credit cards, whose overseers invariably ended up calling Edward, who then called Daisy, who in turn refused his help no matter how much he pleaded "for the children's sake."

And so when she arrived home that day, having deposited Tasha at ballet, she was surprised to see Jorge, the gardener, waiting at the front door.

"Jorge!" she said.

"Mrs. Hillman," he said.

"It's not Tuesday, is it?"

"No, ma'am," he said. "It's just you haven't paid me in three months."

"Oh my God!" she cried, "I'm so sorry! Come in and I'll write you a check. Next time just ask me sooner."

"It's all right, ma'am," he said. "No problem. It's just, you know, three months."

Jorge spoke in a thick accent that she assumed was Mexican but actually was Guatemalan, and she barely understood anything he said, particularly when it came to what he was doing in the garden, so she got in the habit of nodding amiably whenever he spoke. It was because of this that she was shocked at the size of the bill, since it reflected the purchase of quite a few trees, shrubs, and perennials, on top of the work it took to remove a troublesome redwood and a rotten live oak.

"Jorge," she said, "I'm just renting here. All these purchases—"

"Eh?" he said.

"I'm just a renter. We don't do improvements like that."

"Renter?"

"You know, I don't own this house."

"No?"

"No."

"Ah," he said.

"I thought it was just part of the monthly fee, all those plants."

"You want me to take them out?" he asked.

"What?"

"You want me to take them out?"

"No, we don't need to go out. I know what's out there."

"No, take them to garbage." He pantomimed carrying a huge load and tossing it toward the street.

"Oh, *throw* them out. But I'd still have to pay for them, wouldn't I?"

"You can't take that stuff back."

"What?"

"You can't take that stuff back."

"Yes, the stuff in the back."

"*Sí*," he said.

"Okay, look, I'll just write you a check for all this. But no more planting without telling me."

"I do tell you," he said.

"What?"

"Yeah, okay," he said. "No more."

"*No más*," she said.

"Right. *No más*," he replied.

She sighed at the impossibility of ever really communicating with anyone, even a gardener she'd had for years whom everyone said spoke perfect English. Suddenly she recalled the missed phone call in the car and realized it must have been Edward wanting to rescue her again, but not without first making her feel like an idiot. She fished her checkbook out of her purse and scribbled her signature as fast as she could, mumbling the whole time, "Jorge, I'm so embarrassed, I really am. It won't happen again."

"It's okay," said Jorge. "No problem, really."

"You're very kind, Jorge," she said.

"Lots of people forget to pay," he said.

"They do?"

"Sure."

"Jorge," she suddenly said, "come in and have a cup of tea."

"Oh, no," he said.

"Please."

He fiddled with the check.

"Please," she said. "Please."

Eventually he followed her past the Christmas tree with its dozens of presents piled beneath its emerald limbs and into her tiny kitchen, which the landlord had refurbished with bright blue IKEA cabinets. She sat him down at the counter and turned on the electric kettle.

"What kind of tea do you like?" she asked.

He offered her a blank smile.

"I have all kinds. In black tea, I have Yunnan and Darjeeling, and I have chai and chamomile and Mighty Leaf Green Dragon. I have oolong if you like oolong, or rooibos—Would you like rooibos?"

"Please, you choose."

"I like mango blend."

"Okay," he said.

"But you can have whatever you want."

"That's good."

"What is?"

"What you said. That one." He pointed to the tea bags in her hand.

She was disappointed, of course, because she wanted him to feel comfortable and equal and she knew he didn't. She had put him in an awkward situation and now she regretted this. She hadn't meant at all to humiliate him—just the opposite, in fact. But there was no way to stop it now—that would have been far worse. So she put a mango-blend tea bag in his cup and a mango-blend tea bag in her own cup, and when the water was ready she poured first his, then hers, and then she sat down next to him on the stool and said, "Sugar? Sweetener? Milk? Lemon?"

"Sugar," he said, and she handed him the bowl and he put a tiny bit into his tea, though she knew, just knew, he really liked a lot of sugar.

"Take as much as you like," she said.

"Thank you," he said, but didn't take any more.

"Be careful, it's hot," she said.

"Okay, thank you," he said.

Then they sat side by side for some minutes without speaking, and also without drinking, because the tea really was too hot, and finally Daisy asked him about his family and he told her everyone was fine and she asked about his eldest daughter, Estrella, and he said she was in college now and when Daisy heard the word "college" she said, "You must be very proud," and he nodded, and then he began to tell her about his son, Antonio, and how he loved computers and wanted to make computer games, but that he would probably go into the army first because that way his education would be paid for, and also a little about Esme, his youngest, who just entered high school, who was very beautiful and had to be careful, but that everyone was fine, just fine.

"I'm glad," she said, assuming from his tone and also the word "fine" that everything at home was going well.

And then she asked him the question she had wanted to ask him from the first, which was, "Why didn't you call Mr. Hillman about the bill? Everyone else does."

"Oh," he said, "I'm very sorry! I offended you—"

"No, no, don't be alarmed," she told him. "I'm glad you didn't."

"I don't know," he said, staring into his teacup, "I thought you want to be the one to pay."

"Why?"

"I don't know. It seems it is important to you. To do it yourself."

She made out only half of what he said, but what she pieced together made her happy.

"You're very sensitive," she said to him.

"Sorry?"

"You are very kind."

"No, no," he said.

"Yes, yes," she said. She broke into a warm smile, then went to the pantry and produced some cookies, which she put on a plate. She herself took the first bite, and the chocolate was still on her teeth when she laughed and said, "See? There is some sweetness in this world, isn't there?"

Jorge took his own bite of cookie. "For sure," he said.

"You think a person can change, don't you, Jorge?"

"Yes," he said. "A person can change."

"I think I've changed," she went on. "I think I'm starting to be my own person."

They drank a few more sips of tea; then Jorge stood up and looked at his watch.

"I'm sorry, Mrs. Hillman," he said. "Another house."

"Of course, of course, I'm sorry to have kept you so long."

She led him to the door.

"You probably think I'm crazy," she said.

"No, Mrs. Hillman. You are a very nice lady."

"I wish everyone thought that."

She could see how desperate he was to leave, but still she could not let him go.

"Jorge," she said, "it's really okay that you planted all that stuff in the yard. You make everything so beautiful, and you were just following your instinct. How were you supposed to know we didn't own this house?"

"Yeah, I didn't know."

"Some people just make the world more beautiful, Jorge. They can't help themselves."

"Good-bye, Mrs. Hillman."

"Yes, of course, good-bye, Jorge."

"Thank you, Mrs. Hillman."

"You're welcome. We'll do it again some time."

"Thank you," he said. "Bye-bye."

"Okay, 'bye," she said.

"Bye-bye," he said, and almost ran down the driveway to his truck.

Daisy closed the door and went back inside. The clock in the hallway chimed four fifteen. She'd have to pull herself together and go back for Tasha, she was already late. She guessed she wouldn't talk to the instructor today. It was too much. She heard Jorge drive off and had to ask herself what on earth was she thinking, asking him in for tea? What had she wanted from him? She decided she had better look over her bills and pay them tonight. But for now, she just stared out the rear window at the fading light and Jorge's beautiful plantings—azalea in wild clumps, hydrangea growing up along the back fence, roses, some of which were amazingly still in bloom, hibiscus waiting out the winter, lantanas in full color, and several trees— she recognized juniper and manzanita and Japanese maple in various states of sleep or growth. She held the teacup within her two hands, held it close to her chest where she might feel the heat radiate through her palms and into her body, and enjoyed the steam rushing up to her nostrils rich with the scent of mango.

She was in love. There was nothing she could do about it. Edward would never have been able to stand up to that love and neither had Noah, the most recent boyfriend, and most likely no one else would, either. But she would have to try. Surely Henry Quantum wasn't the only man in the world for her. Surely that kind of thing was nonsense—the idea that there was only one soul in the entire universe destined for you, preordained by God—as if God cared. But if God exists, she thought, then she must care. She must care for each and every one of us. Or else she wouldn't be God, would she?

Henry's face came up to greet her in the steam rising from the teacup and in the bloom of those errant roses and in her own reflection in the glass of her kitchen window. And everything suddenly seemed rather beautiful to her.

Her garden was beautiful, the grass pushing up between the faded brick path, the dark earth holding fast the bulbs that slept within, the fat blue jay fluttering merrily in the waxen lemon tree—so lovely! And the photograph of herself with her two children taken on Mount Tam near the cataracts, the silver rush of waters cascading behind them, that, too, was beautiful; and the copper pots hanging from hooks in her kitchen, these also were beautiful. And so was the scent Jorge left behind, and the faint aroma of fir drifting in from the living room, and the way the maple shivered in the wind that had suddenly come up from the sea, and—

"Oh!" she cried. "It's raining!"

The rain on the window and the tears in her eyes turned everything into a kaleidoscope of colors shrouded in a forest of mist. The clock struck four thirty. She rummaged through the hall closet for her raincoat, found the umbrella, and went out to the car to pick up her daughter at dance class.

PART FOUR

HENRY

CHAPTER 12

December 23rd, 4:17–5:49 p.m.

He'd been sitting in Union Square still thinking about whether there was actual space between atoms or if distance was an illusion and we were all holograms projected from the edge of some black hole of a universe, when the downpour came—hard and cold and sudden and without warning. Right before he'd left, Santa had asked him what he wanted for Christmas and for some reason Henry blurted out "Rain!" And Santa said, "Well, you've been a good boy this year, so, okay." And fifteen minutes later—*pow*! Henry had to laugh out loud. He raised his arms wide and opened his mouth as far as it would go so he might feel and drink every drop of that glorious rain as it fell on his face and hands.

That lasted a good five seconds.

He ran to find shelter at Emporio Rulli, but the tiny café was overflowing with tourists who were also trying to stay dry. There was a great deal of pushing and shoving, in fact, and the panicked faces of the waiters reminded Henry of movies he'd seen about prison riots—so he gave up on Emporio Rulli (and their wonderful Italian pastries, which he'd been thinking about for the last half hour at least) and decided he had no choice but to get seriously wet. Thus he made his way out of the square and over to the St. Francis hotel, where he thought he might at least be able to catch a cab back to the office—but of course it was a madhouse there as well. As if they'd never seen rain before. And this made him wonder, as he squeezed himself through the throng under the wrought-iron awning of the hotel entrance, if rainwater gets into our brains and washes away all knowledge of past storms. What, after all, would be so horrible if we got a little wet? What are we so afraid of? Well, of course, we're all afraid of something, and maybe when it rains those fears are somehow activated. Because in wetness there are no boundaries—by which he meant, water had no outline, not unless you captured it in a bottle, and so when it rained and the bottle of heaven broke, or, at best, leaked, everyone was reminded that their bodies are bottles, too: just paper-thin membranes of skin holding in all that liquid, and if *we* began leaking, why, we'd bleed to death. Rain is just another way of saying your life is hanging by a thread.

But we need this rain, he thought. It's a blessing! Thank God, thank God, for this rain! Unless of course you're on vacation. Then it sucks.

The doorman's whistle brought Henry out of his reverie long enough for him to shout over the general mayhem, "I'd be happy to share a cab with anyone! I'm just going to Jackson Square." But none of the tourists knew where Jackson Square was and certainly had no desire to go there, and even when Henry reached into his wallet and waved some largish bills about, the doorman ignored him. Fate, Henry understood, was knocking. And his fate was not to score a cab. Henry steeled his heart, assured himself that rain was not really a symbol of chaos, muttered in a cool, low voice, "How much wetter can I get than I already am?" and leapt out into the blustering wild that was the corner of Post and Powell. Thus, ignoring the crowds surging along with their shopping bags over their heads, not to mention the cars splattering mud on all who came too close to the curb, and disregarding the stinging nettle of rain that slapped his cheeks and pricked his eyes, he commenced his trek back to Bigalow, Green, Anderson and Silverman.

But he was wrong. He could indeed get wetter. In fact, there seemed to be no end to how wet he could get. It wasn't the end of the world, though, because having entirely forgotten why he had gone downtown in the first place, he now saw himself as a lone pioneer crossing some unmapped, windswept plain, an explorer braving the torrential white waters of the San Francisco Amazon, a mountaineer ascending the Chinatown Annapurna without so much as a down parka or a pair of mittens, a ragged, bone-thin *ʒek* escaping the Union Square gulag with only a Muni Metro pass as his guide! No, Henry Quantum was not one to be afraid of a little rain. And something else happened, too. He noticed how the tourists and shoppers had disappeared, as if evaporated into the clouds, and he was finally alone, face-to-face with his great city. He had always loved San Francisco, loved it in his bones. But now, slopping through puddles and slipping here and there on a manhole or a sewer grate, he saw his town with new eyes.

He had more or less retraced his steps through Chinatown, first along Grant Avenue and then up Pacific, emerging at the five corners where Pacific meets Columbus and Kearny. To his right he spotted the black and white sign of Bask, the tapas place, and to his left the wan neon lights of Tosca Cafe, where once he had seen Baryshnikov holding forth with friends over spiked cappuccinos, and up on Kearny, though he couldn't yet glimpse it, he knew Tommaso's was waiting, much loved for its calzone even though the place had been there forever, and across from that would be the Lusty Lady with the nipples that lit up at night—though it might have closed—so maybe he was thinking of the Hustler Club or the Hungry I or the Garden of Eden—it really didn't matter. They were all equally and unrepentantly and gloriously seedy.

And right around the corner from where he stood, the rain still cascading off his head, his socks being so wet that little puddles were forming under his toes, and his scarf a soggy rag around his chin, was the original Brandy Ho's Hunan, which, by the way, was still great, and, down on Columbus where Zim's used to be was the Cafe Zoetrope, which Francis Ford Coppola owned. It was situated in the Flatiron Building, which Coppola also owned but used to be owned by the Kingston Trio and in which one of Henry's art director friends once had an office—a guy who did the best storyboards he ever saw, but then he died in a skiing accident and everyone forgot all about him.

He sighed for his lost friend, and when he did, water poured into his mouth and he almost choked. He didn't care—it was just so sad. Everyone forgot him! In fact, he himself couldn't bring the guy's name to mind at the moment, though he knew it would come to him probably at four in the morning when it no longer mattered. His poor, dead friend would never again taste the onion cakes at the House of Nanking, which was also right around the corner, and it had been his favorite place. He stifled another sigh so as not to get another mouthful of water—but this sigh was for himself, because he knew that someday his presence would also be obliterated and the city—his city—would go on without him, too. House of Nanking will go on, Tommaso's will go on, but Henry Quantum will not.

Oh, he was filled with grief! Filled with the San Francisco he would no longer inhabit! Just down the block was the Comstock Saloon, which used to be something else, but he still liked the beer there. And Mr. Bing's, which in all his years he never entered because he assumed only Chinese gangsters were supposed to go there, but jeez, that bar must have been around since the fifties at least, and "Bing's" doesn't even sound Chinese, so he decided then and there that this was his year to get a drink at Mr. Bing's!

Yes, he was filled to the brim with San Francisco, with its eternal beauty and bounty—a city without boundaries, a beacon to all who did not fear the rain—and he was happy now that it would go on without him.

When he finally arrived at the office, Gladys was putting on her coat and fishing an old umbrella out of the closet.

"Bones! Where the hell have you been? Everyone was looking for you."

"I guess I was buying perfume," he said.

"I tried to reach you on your cell. Honestly!"

"Sorry," he said.

"So where's the perfume?" She gestured at his empty hands.

"Oh," he shrugged, "I guess I forgot."

"Forgot?"

"Something came up."

"It always does. But I have to tell you, Mr. Bigalow was concerned."

"Why?"

"You missed a planning meeting."

"I did?"

"Year-end wrap-up. It was in your calendar."

"No, I don't think so."

"Bones, everyone's calendar is automatically updated."

"Okay, I'll talk to him."

"Too late. He's gone home. And look at you. You're sopping wet!"

"Yeah," he said, "I guess I am."

"I don't know why you even own a cell phone," she said.

"You sound like my wife."

"Maybe she has a point," Gladys replied.

He looked at her now, really for the first time—the bouncy ponytail, the toned athletic body in the tailored skirt and pink cashmere V-neck, the smooth bronze skin, the arms napped in auburn down, and saw that, in spite of her cool, aristocratic air, she was the most ordinary creature on earth.

"It's only rain," he said.

"Right. That's why we have umbrellas."

She slipped out of her heels and tied on a pair of running shoes.

"Don't forget to lock the door behind you," she said. "You're the last." Then she smiled politely, as always, and disappeared down the stairs.

Henry waited until he heard the outer door close and only then strolled down the hall to his digs. It was as good to be alone in the office as it was to be a trailblazer on the stormy streets. He'd spent so much time in this place, but when had he ever been alone? Slowly he made his way past the empty desks and silent file cabinets, the copy machine that for once sat sleeping, the art directors' tools that had found their way back into their compartments, the computers that had retreated into their own mysterious cyberspace, the conference rooms filled only with empty chairs: they all seemed quite content to be without their human masters. To tell the truth, he told himself, we all could just as easily work at home, couldn't we? Connect by Skype or whatever. But somehow no. People have to congregate. Like colonies of yeast coagulating on the side of a test tube. What, though, he wondered, is the reason for all this propinquity?

And then it came to him. *Gluons!*

He had read about gluons. It was another quantum problem, maybe the very essence of the quantum problem. To understand a gluon (he explained to his imaginary and rapt class of physics-impaired copywriters), you first have to understand protons and quarks: a proton, which contains a good deal of the mass of an atom (neutrons supply most of the rest), is made up of three quarks. But quarks have almost no mass at all, even though they make up most of the proton. So where does the mass come from? It's supposed to be supplied by something called a gluon. But guess what? The gluons have no mass of their own, either! They pop in and out of existence in far less than a blink of an eye, and although they seem to take up space, they don't! This (dear amazed and totally mesmerized students) is the crazy universe we live in! But gluons *do* have a purpose even if they're not really there. And that is: to glue the whole proton together—i.e., *glu*-on. Not with glue, he chuckled to his wide-eyed audience, but with a remarkable and, I would posit, *satanic* force. For here is the disturbing part: even though the impulse of a quark is to move away from other quarks—to get out of that damned proton as fast as it can— the gluon won't let it. In fact, the farther one quark drifts from another, the stronger the force between them, just the opposite of gravity. Which means the poor little quark can't flee. No matter how hard it tries, no matter how much it wants its freedom, it will *never* get away from the other quarks. That is a fundamental law of quantum physics. A quark is stuck to its partners no matter what it wants for itself.

"Stuck," he said, only half realizing that he was moaning at the same time. "Totally, completely, one hundred percent stuck!"

He considered the empty conference room. Tomorrow it would be filled with staff anxiously awaiting their Christmas bonuses before heading off to the party at MoMo's. He would be one of them. He would open his envelope and feel justly rewarded for selling products no one wanted or needed; rewarded and also emasculated. That envelope was the gluon. And none of us would ever escape, because the harder we tried, the farther we fled, the more strength it had to pull us back. And not just the money. But the whole thing. The whole need to congregate. To be part of something. To have a place in this world. To succeed no matter what.

He sat himself down, kicked the nearest chair, and watched it roll into the one beside it. It doesn't feel a thing, he thought. Not a thing. He could take an ax to that chair and it wouldn't know the difference. And yet if he did chop it into firewood he'd certainly get fired. Because we hold these objects, these nothings, more dear than we do actual, living people.

It was the whole capitalist system! He was just an ox yoked to a millstone!

And naturally this made him think about Genghis Khan.

Because when Genghis was a boy he was shackled to a stone yoke. Had he not escaped he would have been executed when he'd grown to the height of a wagon wheel. He ran hundreds of miles with that yoke around his neck to get away. At least he did in the movie. But Henry Quantum understood Genghis Khan very well. Because poor Genghis never did get away. He carried that yoke all his life. That's why he extracted so cruel a vengeance, a vengeance such as the world had never seen.

Do I want vengeance? wondered Henry Quantum. Not really. It only makes things worse. And who wants that?

Because on a macro level, on the level of thermodynamics, which he had to admit he only barely comprehended, things were quite opposite of all those gluons and quarks. Here an idea called entropy ruled—being the tendency of objects in nature to fall apart. And guess what? Entropy is called the *strong force*. And that which binds things together? The *weak force*. And what is it that binds people together? Why, love. Love binds people together. Love is the weakest force of all.

He sighed and said to himself, "How many sighs can a person sigh in one fucking day?"

He might as well have asked how many stars are in the galaxy and how many galaxies are in the universe and how many universes are in the multiverse. Because that's how many sighs are in a day.

And maybe entropy is also why everyone comes to work. Because every attachment is ephemeral, because we really are just representations of data on the edge of a black hole, because love is useless and it's better to settle for an illusion than to have nothing at all. The truth is, if you make a decent commercial for Protox, maybe you won't notice the entropy for another half hour and maybe your customer won't, either. That's not such a bad thing, is it? Although what could have more entropy than Protox? It's a fucking laxative. At least it won't kill you like Samurai Brand Real Beef Chewing Jerky and Pinch of Beef.

"You still here?"

He looked up. It was Denise, the art director.

"Oh, hi. I thought I was alone. I was just thinking about things," he said.

"You should know better than to do that. You look positively suicidal."

"Do I?"

"All crumpled. And you're incredibly wet."

"I got caught in the rain."

Denise wrapped her long, languid fingers around his arm and drew him up. "Come with me," she said.

She led him through the hall to the bathroom and pulled a wad of paper towels from the dispenser. "Here," she said. "Dry your hair. And take off your jacket, and—oh man, strip off that shirt. We can dry it on the hand dryer. T-shirt, too."

He did as he was told.

"And check out your pants, man," she said. "They are seriously gross."

"What can I do?" he asked.

"Dude," she held out her hand, "just give them to me."
When he didn't, she stepped forward and unhooked his belt.
"Hey, man, you're not, like, going to make me do the rest,
are you?"

"No, no," he said. He slid them off and held them out
to her.

She laughed. "Henry Quantum! I wouldn't have expected it, but you have a pretty decent body. It's cool you
don't work out. I like the no-abs thing."

"Thank you."

She laughed again. "Do you always have to be polite?"

"Was that wrong?"

"No. It's cute."

"Thank you," he said.

She laughed once more.

"Sorry," he said.

She hung his trousers over the stall and asked, "You like
me, don't you?"

"Of course I like you."

"No, I mean, like, you *like* me."

"I—Well—"

"It might surprise you to know I like you, too."

"Me?"

"Yes, you."

She tapped his nose with her forefinger, that eel-like forefinger with the black-enameled nail that curved ever so slightly inward like a Chinese empress's.

"We're completely alone," she said. "The place is ours."

"Uh . . ." he said.

"You know that a lot of girls like you," she continued. "There's something about you. I mean, aside from the cluelessness, which I have to admit, I find attractive. You don't put on airs. You don't judge. I like that. I like that you treat people so nicely. Like Schwartz. He's a complete douche. You know he's a douche. I know he's a douche. But you are kind to him anyway. You don't even notice how kind you are. And that cowlick or whatever it's called—you always have some hair sticking up out of place. It's cute, that's all. You kind of look like Cary Grant, when he played the nutty professor."

One had to admit, Denise was extremely beautiful in her strangeness, in the wild colors of her hair and the feather extensions that seemed so exotic to him, in the boyish body with those tiny breasts with their razor-sharp nipples that all of the guys remarked upon on a daily basis because they were almost always visible beneath her skimpy blouses and clingy sweaters, a beautiful boyish body made the more so by the skintight floral pants and the Western shirt with its

embroidered collar and pearl snaps and the sleeves ripped off at the shoulders to expose tattoos of snakes and flowers and strange geometries in blue and red and brown and green that ran all the way down to her wrists and ended in a single tendril of ivy that curled along the back of her hands. He knew a lot of people thought she was gay, and in fact she once told him that she sometimes was, but apparently she wasn't today; and though it was true that her face was a bit boyish with its large, hard features, the softness of her mouth, and the way her bottom lip protruded like a little cup, and the musky insinuation of her voice, which matched the musky insinuation of her scent, didn't seem boyish at all.

"Are my pants dry yet?" he asked

"I just hung them up, Henry. So I doubt it. Anyway, what's the rush?"

"No rush. It's just—"

"Don't you like me?"

"Of course I like you. It's just, you know, I have my pants off."

"I think we've already established that."

"Oh," he said.

The whole of Denise seemed to be made of liquid rubber. She had no edges at all. Tall, gangly, bony, yet structureless. She was like some strange amorphous sea creature

that slithers along the ocean floor and he watched with some alarm as her jellylike hand slid from the tip of his nose down to his bare chest, found his nipples and squeezed them like she might two ripe plums in the market. She smiled one of her Mona Lisa smiles.

That's also when he noticed her other hand had gone all the way down to his groin, where it clamped on to what it found there like an octopus engulfing its pray.

"Merry Christmas, Bones!" she chimed.

"Uh . . ." he said.

CHAPTER 13

5:50–9:03 p.m.

What a crazy day this had been! He was blown away, simply blown away at how things had turned out and also at himself and at life and at all the good and bad that had been thrown in his direction. But for better or worse, everything having happened as it happened, he put his clothes back on and left the office as quickly as he could, saying to Denise that he really had to pick up his brother-in-law right away, which wasn't precisely true, because the flight wasn't due for an hour and a half. He was a little surprised that Denise didn't mind, in fact she laughed that same mocking, affectionate laugh. Unfortunately she had never gotten around to using the hand dryer on his shirt or on anything else, so his clothes were still filthy, soaked, and freezing. He spotted his reflec-

THE HEART OF HENRY QUANTUM

tion in the office window. He looked like he'd been dragged though the mud by a pickup truck. He was okay with that, all things considered.

This time, though, he grabbed an umbrella—he always kept one propped near the trash can—and bid Denise good-bye with a rather chaste wave of his hand. He made his way out onto the street, bent his umbrella into the wind, and pushed on to the garage on Battery Street. Roberto was still there behind his little podium and when Henry saw him, he waved happily.

"I guess the drought is over," said Roberto. "You can rest easy now."

"One rain doesn't end a drought," he clucked.

"But it's a good start, yes?"

"Yes it is. Yes it is!"

Henry liked Roberto. Roberto was unchanging, solid as the promontories that held up the Golden Gate Bridge; each morning and night he was a kind of marker in the stormy sea of Henry's life. But he'd forgotten to give Roberto his Christmas bonus, and only now did he realize this, and even though Roberto was his usual smiling self, Henry worried that this rock might falter if its feelings were hurt; and also Henry just enjoyed making Roberto happy. For some reason, he was always telling Roberto jokes. He set down his umbrella, took out his checkbook and wrote out a Christmas bonus right then and there, quite a large one, larger than he had planned upon, and Roberto thanked him effusively, saying, "Please, please, Mr. Quantum, it's not necessary," and handed Henry a little cellophane package of chocolates, exclaiming, "For our special customers only!" Henry cried with delight, "Really?" and then the two of them wished each other merry Christmas and Roberto fetched the BMW 528i, which, when it arrived, thrilled Henry as always, and Roberto said, "I filled it up for you," and Henry swelled with self-satisfaction and well-being because there was nothing like having a full tank, and again they wished each other Merry Christmas, and Henry drove off thinking that at least there was one relationship in his life he could count on.

It occurred to him that even though the universe definitively works toward entropy, and unquestionably time and distance are arrayed against us in the most profound ways, still, there are things that make you feel like there is some meaning in all this. And maybe if love wasn't possible, friendship at least was. It's the little things we do, he decided—having a younger woman take off your pants, for instance, or having a good garage guy, or having a nice chat with Santa Claus—that's what counts. Sure, you can look at all this as our pathetic attempt to avoid the cosmic void, but you can also see it as—he pondered for a moment—Zen sand painting!

Exactly! Look how carefully, how exquisitely the Zen master works, how ardent he is in the perfection of his technique, how profoundly moving is the beauty of his design, and yet the first wind that comes along—*poof*—it's all gone. And he welcomes that! He welcomes that wind. A true Zen master will not even photograph his sand painting. Why? Because that would utterly miss the point! And the point is: in this evanescent, impermanent, and utterly dark world, great beauty is not only possible, it is essential. This was such a heartening revelation that Henry Quantum almost came to tears. For even though the rain was clouding his windshield and the fog was obscuring the road ahead, he saw the truth clear as day: nothing beautiful is in vain.

By the time he had finished thinking this, he was already on King Street, having circled the Embarcadero, and was about to go up the ramp to the freeway toward the airport. In spite of the weather, traffic was moving quickly. He supposed people had finally had time to get used to the rain, or maybe it was just that nobody but idiots like him went to work so near to Christmas. Anyway, Henry decided to relax and enjoy the scent of his leather seats and the fresh zest of ozone coming through his slightly open window.

Maybe he should call Margaret, he thought. But when she was meeting with a client she never picked up. She was always yelling at him about not answering his phone, but she was just as bad. Although it seemed to him she always managed to answer everyone else's calls.

He so wanted to understand what was going on between himself and Margaret.

He recalled the first apartment they'd shared in North Beach—it was huge by their standards then—and the rent was four hundred a month, a fortune! The ceilings had been sprayed with sparkling foam—he laughed now recalling how they used to lie in bed looking at that ceiling, gathering clusters of sparkles into constellations that they named according to their mood: the constellation Sexpot, the constellation Pasta, and one of their favorites, the constellation Shakespeare, which meant it was time to read aloud from the sonnets. Did they actually do that? Or did he just imagine it? Or maybe it happened only once and he transformed it into something more. He had no way of knowing: only that thinking these things, remembering these things, created a painful longing in him. And yet he knew it was not for Margaret he longed—not even the Margaret of those days, if she ever existed. Perhaps he used to wish for those days to return, but not anymore.

Even so, he hadn't wanted an affair. For years he'd been living in the shadow of Margaret's indifference, waiting for the light to return, which sometimes it did in little flashes that might illuminate a walk or an evening at home. But the main light never did return, and when Daisy appeared, how could he avoid naming that darkness and running toward the flame Daisy held out to him?

He swung onto the feeder road to the airport, followed the directions to short-term parking, and found a space near the green signs for United. It was amazing Margaret had gotten Arthur on a flight so quickly. It was two days before Christmas—who gets a last-minute flight right before Christmas? She probably had to put him in first class, full fare. Yes, Margaret seemed to own the world, while he, Henry, simply observed. What, he wondered, had he done to make her hate him so? He walked from the garage to the terminal and ended up at the foot of the escalator in baggage claim where you were allowed to meet disembarking passengers.

Arthur's flight was scheduled to arrive at 7:12. It was now 6:30, but weather had caused a delay and his flight wasn't due until 7:50. Almost an hour and half. Henry could hear his feet squeaking in his wet shoes. He ran his fingers though his hair—flat as a pancake and still a little damp. He tucked in his shirt, looked down at the mud on his cuffs, and thought: I must look like a lunatic. No wonder people are keeping clear of me. Maybe I should buy some clothes. He looked around. There was a Starbucks kiosk just past the carousels. No help there. Perhaps he could just look nonchalant. One hand in his pocket. Casual stance. Ralph Lauren.

Or maybe it would be better if he took a walk.

He made his way up to the departure section, which, unlike arrivals, was a bit more open to the public. There were a couple of shops before you got to security, but they were for candy and the like. He thought he might just saunter for a while. That's it, saunter. What a nice word. Saunter. Thoreau liked that word. What had he said? To appear to be going on pilgrimage but never quite getting there. That was Thoreau. That was sauntering. In fact, Henry had memorized a great deal of Thoreau in his youth, along with Keats and Chaucer, Shakespeare and Milton. He knew parts of the *Iliad* by heart, too, and Eliot, and quite a few Basho haiku, and could even quote from Marx once upon a time, so he was pleased that he could now recall, at least vaguely, what Thoreau had to say about sauntering. It came from the Middle Ages, in the time of the Crusades, when vagabonds used to roam the countryside begging for money to help them on their journey to *la sainte terr*—yes, that was it! Henry gleefully patted himself on the back. But everyone knew they weren't really going to the Holy Land, just to the nearest tavern, so the children used to chide them, calling out, "There goes a *sainte terrer*!" That's right: a saunterer! A Holy Lander! But the truth is, nobody knows how to walk, really walk. You have to have a genius for it: and that's called sauntering. The point is to just walk, walk in a way whose end is the walk itself, and your intention is nothing but to be on that walk and to experience everything you can on that walk in the moment in which it occurs—then you really *are* going to the Holy Land, because you bring that Holy Land right along with you.

And that, Henry declared to himself, is more or less what I've been doing all day. And indeed, now when he examined his clothes, he thought: Thoreau would approve! I may look like a bum but I'm not a bum. I'm a saunterer.

Poor Margaret! When was the last time she took a real walk?

And that is why once again the idea came into his mind: perfume!

Why don't I just get that fucking perfume here and save another trip downtown? Surely there were places in the airport where you could buy a lady an ounce of perfume.

Unfortunately, a quick perusal of the departure area proved that all the good stuff was beyond the security station sequestered behind rows of X-ray machines and phalanxes of security guards. He supposed he could buy himself a ticket to somewhere cheap, say to Burbank, go through security, buy the perfume, and hightail it back out. All he needed was a refundable ticket. On the other hand, if he was given a boarding pass in order to pass through security, would they still give him his money back? And if he didn't get on the plane, wouldn't they assume he was a terrorist? Come to his house in the middle of the night and make him disappear? And even if none of that happened, wouldn't he be holding up the flight until they were sure he hadn't put any luggage on it? He wouldn't like it if someone had done that to him. Especially on Christmas. Not to mention that by the time he bought a ticket and gone back and forth and all that, Arthur's flight would have arrived, he'd be waiting in a state of confusion and panic, and then there'd be hell to pay from Margaret. When he thought of Margaret's anger, he decided he better check the arrivals monitor again, just in case.

Arthur's plane had been delayed another half hour.

He began his saunter again, determined to notice even more detail than before: the design of the carpet, which was ghastly; the way the arrival and departure monitors were hung, which was inconvenient; the placement of the little waiting areas, which were too small and too near the doors. I am really sauntering this time, he delighted in telling himself. It occurred to him that perhaps he had concluded too quickly that there were no stores this side of security, so he continued along, only now with a renewed objective, which interfered with the purity of his sauntering, but just like in meditation, you go in and out, in and out. He decided it was okay to saunter with an objective—Chanel No. 5—because he'd had the same objective that morning and look where it took him.

He soon found himself entering a rather long passageway, which he followed even though there were very few people in it, and when he came to the end he was surprised to find he had emerged in the international terminal. Here everything was very modern and streamlined and much less crowded, and also the restaurants were available to anyone, not just the ticketed passengers, and, though he didn't see any, Henry assumed there were shops aplenty, and surely one that carried Chanel No. 5. It was a vast space with soaring ceilings and marble floors, and around him he heard many languages, not just Spanish or Chinese. It suddenly occurred to him how marvelous a thing language is. After all, who first pointed to a chicken and said "chicken"? And who was the other guy who said, "Yeah, that's a chicken all right." Or did they first come up with the word "bird"? Did the organizing concept of birdhood come before or after chickens? In fact, how is it that one thing stands for another—that a word can substitute for a thing or that at some point the word becomes the thing, even surpasses the thing—like "love." The word "love" is so much more solid, more tangible, more comprehensible than the actual experience of love. In reality, love is nothing but confusion and despair with a little ecstasy thrown in. But *say* the word "love" and immediately you think of *Romeo and Juliet* or *Doctor Zhivago* or *Brokeback Mountain*—and everyone seems to know what you are talking about, and yet to live through love is to know nothing at all.

Oh, the human heart, he wailed, the greatest mystery of all! Of course it's the brain really, not the heart. The trillions of synapses and infinite lines of possibility. Isn't that what Daisy was studying? How a photon of light becomes a picture in your brain. How we take this crazy world inside us and make it understandable?

But he didn't want to think about Daisy.

Although it was Daisy he was thinking about when he said no to Denise. Actually he'd said, "I'm married, I can't," but it wasn't Margaret who'd come into his mind. It was Daisy with her flurry of red hair and her sparkling gold-green eyes and the freckles on her delicate, energetic hands.

"Oh, come on," Denise had said.

"I can't," he insisted.

"No one will know."

"I'll know."

She pressed herself up against him and whispered, "Yes, you will."

Maybe because they were in the bathroom, maybe because it was the office, maybe because it was Christmas— but mostly because of those few moments he had spent with Daisy at lunch—he said, "Gotta go!"

And he grabbed his sopping clothes, ran naked into his office, dressed with the speed of Superman in a phone booth, and ran out to the street and all the way to the garage before he realized he'd left his sports coat in the bathroom.

Now, however, he reminded himself: perfume. So he recommenced his search of the international terminal in earnest. There was a very elegant food court, with two sushi bars and a really nice steak house and yet another Emporio

Rulli café as well as the usual newsstands and bookshops; he even found a place where he could take a shower—they sold toiletries, but no Chanel No. 5—and there was a Brookstone where he couldn't resist the massage chair and thought about buying one (for Margaret of course) even though it was three thousand dollars, but the guy said it was too late to get it delivered by Christmas, so he nixed that idea, and later he walked by one of those places where you could rent a DVD player, not that anyone did anymore, and thought about how he and Margaret used to watch Netflix movies together, but now they just downloaded onto their own devices and sat separated by headphones and personal taste. Finally there was a museum shop, but it was closed, and even though he spent quite awhile with his nose pressed against their window, he knew that even if it had been open, there would have been no perfume.

He sighed. He tried not to, but he couldn't help it, because he saw in his mind's eye Margaret dabbing Chanel No. 5 on her clavicle, and this grieved him. Maybe that's why he thought of perfume in the first place. Because when he thought about perfume, he always thought about Margaret and about her dabbing it on her clavicle and also behind her ears and upon her wrists—and how he delighted in coming up behind her, placing his hands upon her shoulders and leaning in so as to catch the sweet wild scent of flowers rising from her body—it was one of the few intimacies they still shared. Yes, that's why he was so damned set on getting the perfume. That brief interlude of tenderness, with his hands upon her shoulders. The beauty of her neck as it curved toward her chin, and how he could sometimes see down the back of her dress the swerve of her spine and the amber skin of her shoulder blades and for that sliver of a moment she was once again unaware of her beauty and of her power over him, and in that moment he was once again, at least a little, madly in love with her.

He had told himself he hadn't a clue why things had changed, but that wasn't true. He did know, and he finally allowed himself to call it to mind, because of the perfume, and because he had been thinking of perfume when he told Daisy that he still loved Margaret—he'd been thinking of those rare and perfect moments when he would come up behind her and hold her shoulders and, mostly, when he felt them relax under his grasp as she opened her neck to welcome him.

Of course the change in Margaret took a long time to unfold. But it had become obvious even as early as the fourth or fifth year of their marriage. She was disappointed in him. There, he said it. It happened one day when he saw the doubt creep in her eyes: What was he doing with his life? What did he intend for the two of them? Finally she had to express it: "You're always going on and on and on, but nothing ever comes of it." To prove her wrong he got into advertising, if for no other reason than to show her he could make money. He had wanted to be a writer, but they placed him in account management, and he surprised himself by doing quite well; in fact, he rose quickly—account executive, account supervisor, account director. But then he faltered, ran aground. He did make decent money, yes; but something had gone out of him. He could easily have become a management supervisor and soon after that the director of management. But he'd gone as far as he wanted to go. He couldn't quite say why. Only that he was standing in some sort of doorway that led nowhere. Or maybe it was quicksand. Or maybe—well, who knows? A couple of creative guys did once approach him to start their own shop, but he hemmed and hawed until they gave up on him. And instantly his caché faded. Most everyone began treating him with a measure of contempt not unlike Margaret's. It was barely perceptible, but undeniable. And this, somehow, filtered into his home, exacerbating his problems with his wife.

But it needn't have.

Margaret could not have cared less about management supervisors or new agencies. She despised the idea of advertising from the outset. She wanted more from him, something she called "great things," even if she herself could not articulate what they were. It certainly wasn't money, at least in the beginning. It was something far more difficult. Margaret had wanted a conqueror, a slayer of dragons, a man of the world. What she got was Henry Quantum. And this left her with but one choice. To either live in shame or to transform herself into that man of the world, that slayer of dragons; and so, over time, that is what she did. And the more dragons she laid to rest, the more she came to despise her husband for his weakness. Henry recognized this and could not in his heart disagree. And not just for his weakness. For his fecklessness, his credulity, his indecision, his puzzlement, his absentmindedness, and for all the musings and daydreams and reveries of mind that resulted in his aimless philosophizing. She was right to hate him.

And yet, she did not leave him. This, to Henry, was the greatest mystery of all.

He had told a lot of this to Daisy when they were together. She blinked her eyes many times and finally said, "Henry, you're crazy. There's absolutely nothing wrong with you. That person you're describing? Guess what? It's not you. It's someone she made up."

"Maybe you don't know me very well," he had said.

"Maybe *you* don't know you very well," she replied.

And the thing was, they were both right. He'd become that miserable weakling with Margaret, but with Daisy he was someone else, someone newer and fresher and more powerful, because, frankly, that's exactly the way he felt around her. That's why he'd said to her that terrible night, "No, I don't feel guilty, not one little bit." Then she dumped him.

He wasn't having any luck with the perfume. He looked at his watch again. He'd already killed almost two hours and now he'd have to get back to baggage claim to meet up with Arthur. The thought of Arthur always depressed him. It was weird. Arthur was ten times the fuckup he was. But Margaret loved him. Really loved him.

So it wasn't that Margaret couldn't love. It's just that she didn't love him.

"Merry fucking Christmas," he said to himself.

By this time he had done a full circle of the main hall of the international terminal; he had listened to dozens of unknown languages and heard the loudspeaker announce flights to dozens of exotic places; he'd poked his nose in all the shops, checked out all the restaurants, and now he tried to find his way back to the tunnel that led to the United terminal. It was then, out of the corner of his eye, that he spotted, tucked away behind some glass partitions and a series of advertising banners, a little store called, simply, THINGS. Well, he thought, I can be a few seconds late for fucking Arthur, so he traversed the hall and arrived at the store just as the young Filipino woman began closing the security gate over the entrance.

"Wait!" cried Henry.

"Sorry, sir, we're closing."

"I see, I see, but I just have one question. Do you carry Chanel Number Five?"

"The perfume?"

"Yes, Chanel Number Five."

"Yes, sir, we do, but we're closing."

"You do?"

"But we're closing."

"Please, please, can I come in? It won't take but a minute, I promise."

The woman pointed to her watch. "We're closing."

"Oh, please, please! It's Christmas!" He saw her finger a little gold cross dangling from her neck. "Christmas?" he said again. She rolled her eyes and, still clutching the cross, reluctantly waved him in. And, oh, it was a lovely store! A lovely store with lovely things on lovely shelves. The nice Christian saleslady went directly to the perfume section, pulled open a drawer, and came back to the register with a beautiful bottle of Chanel No. 5.

But looking around, Henry Quantum suddenly understood—he saw what he had really come for. And it wasn't Chanel No. 5.

CHAPTER 14

9:04 p.m.–?

He had tried to call Margaret, he really had. But of course she never answered when she was with a client, so he left her a voice message, and also texted her, and also e-mailed her.

"Margaret," he said, "I'm sorry, but I can't pick up Arthur. He'll have to take a cab or a shuttle. He'll be fine. I don't have his cell number so I left a message for him at the airport—you know, the white courtesy telephone. He'll figure it out. But I just can't take him tonight. And also, Margaret, I've got something I have to do, so I'll be late. I mean, I don't know when I'll be home. I'll explain later. Sorry about this. Okay. 'Bye."

On the text and e-mail he merely wrote: *Hope your meeting going well. Can't pick up A. Left message. Don't know when home.*

Then he deleted the *Hope your meeting going well.* He didn't mean it, so he decided not to say it.

By now Arthur would have arrived anyway, would have gone through his panic, would have called Margaret, who probably *did* answer, or he used his head for once and got into a cab all by himself. Whatever he did, Henry didn't care.

What he did care about was the package in his arms, which was actually not a package. He'd asked the woman to tie a red ribbon around it, which she did.

Then he'd driven like a madman. He'd driven up 280 and down Nineteenth Avenue and along Park Presidio until it fed onto the Golden Gate Bridge, and after the bridge he continued up 101, past Sausalito and Mill Valley and Lark- spur and Corte Madera and up Sir Francis Drake Boulevard, past Greenbrae and Ross and San Anselmo and then down Center Street to Lansdale Station, and then down Lansdale to Baywood Court, just exactly as was indicated on the Google Map on his iPhone.

The entire time, his mind was blank. The only thought he had was to follow the directions of the lady in Google Maps, who spoke so calmly and never fretted if you made a wrong turn or did something stupid. Finally, he parked his car in front of the house and took up the package in his arms. It was a white teddy bear with a red ribbon around its neck. He named it Christmas Bear. The saleswoman had given him a hard time when he told her he no longer wanted the perfume, but he didn't care about that, either. He paid with cash and didn't wait for change.

Now he stood beside his car looking up at Daisy's house. It was so much smaller than her old place, or his place. He remembered something from the poet Milton, something he'd never understood until this very moment. That hell is vast and formless, but heaven is small and contained, a small room, a little house, like this one with its Christmas tree blinking in the window and a warm glow drifting out from the living room. The rain had finally stopped, leaving behind the clean, bright scent of sugar pine and Douglas fir, and above him the stars began to sparkle through the thinning clouds, and the moon, three-quarters full, smiled to see her minions happy again, and Henry Quantum also smiled. Whatever might happen next, he had finally chosen the perfect Christmas gift.

POSTSCRIPT

A Note from the Author

With one or two notable exceptions, every place in this book is real. If you care to, you can walk Henry's walk, drive Margaret's drive, or visit Daisy's house or her kids' schools. If you do decide to follow in Henry's footsteps, you will have the pleasure, as I have, of falling in love with San Francisco, the most magical city in America, and perhaps in the world.

The author would like to gratefully acknowledge the following: Tom Owens, for falling head over heels for Margaret and explaining to her the ins and outs of real estate development; to Dr. Russell Hamer, PhD, for giving Daisy, the girl of his dreams, the inside scoop on molecular eye research; to an old love of mine, my ancient copy of *Zen Flesh, Zen Bones* that includes *The Gateless Gate* transcribed by Nyogen Senzaki and Paul Reps that in turn includes the koan "Lightning Flashes" by Mu-mon, Anchor Books, undated; to Karen Kosztolnyik, my wonderful editor, for her always enthusiastic support and incisive, loving editing, as well as Louise Burke, Jennifer Bergstrom, Jennifer Long, Liz Psaltis, Jennifer Robinson, and Becky Prager at Gallery; to my dear friend, best cheerleader, lover of literature, and brilliant agent, Michael V. Carlisle; and of course to GSG, love of my life, and the one without whom this, and all my other works and days, would be for naught.